Vampire's Hunger

Also by Cynthia Garner

Warriors of the Rift Series

Kiss of the Vampire, Book 1
Secret of the Wolf, Book 2
Into the Rift, Novella
Heart of the Demon, Book 3

Vampire's Hunger

Book 1 of The Awakening Series

CYNTHIA GARNER

New York Boston

Copyright © 2014 by Cindy Somerville

Excerpt from *Vampire's Thirst* copyright © 2014 by Cindy Somerville

Forever Yours

Hachette Book Group

237 Park Avenue, New York, NY 10017

Hachettebookgroup.com

Twitter.com/foreverromance

First published as an ebook and as a print on demand edition: April 2014

Forever Yours is an imprint of Grand Central Publishing.

The Forever Yours name and logo are trademarks of Hachette Book Group, Inc.

The publisher is not responsible for websites (or their content) that are not owned by the

publisher.

The Hachette Speakers Bureau provides a wide range of authors for speaking events. To find out more, go to www.hachettespeakersbureau.com or call (866) 376-6591.

ISBN 978-1-4555-7921-1 (ebook edition)

ISBN 978-1-4555-5770-7 (print on demand edition)

Acknowledgments

To the best critique group on the planet: You are my cheerleaders, my support, my sounding board and my friends. Thank you from the bottom of my heart.

To my editor, Latoya Smith: You always believe in me and I appreciate that more than words can say. Thank you for making my books the best they can be.

To my agent, Susan Ginsburg: You were the first to believe in me and my storytelling, and I'll always be grateful. Thank you for your awesome support.

Finally, to my family: You love me and let me be what I am without apology. I love you all.

Vampire's Hunger

Chapter One

Kimber Treat, one of only a few necromancers licensed by the county of Summit, Ohio, pushed open the door to the Medical Examiner's lab. "You've got a Lazarus for me?" she asked.

"Yep. Let me get 'im." The Chief M.E. swung open the heavy metal door of the cooler, went inside, and within a few seconds wheeled a sheet-covered corpse into the room. As he did, Kimber took stock of her surroundings. A stenographer perched on a stool nearby, her machine in front of her, fingers poised over the keys. Two burly security guards stood ready, just in case. When the investigation into a murder ran cold and the cops had nothing else to go on, they called in a necromancer.

Most of the time the deceased was revived, questions were asked and answered, and the newly revived was put back to his or her eternal rest. But every once in a while the reaction of the deceased to suddenly being cognizant again was confusion that quickly morphed into frenzied panic. The guards were a necessary precaution.

"You sure you're ready for this?" Homicide detective Carson Bishop moved to stand next to her. He loosened his tie and flicked open the top button of his white shirt, then shoved his fists into the front pockets of his slacks. He tipped his chin toward the sheet-covered body on the metal gurney the Chief M.E. placed in front of her. "Half his face is gone."

She glanced at him then looked at the M.E. "He can talk, though, right? His jaws are intact?"

The older man nodded. "Yep. Most of the damage is to the upper half of his face."

"Then there shouldn't be a problem. Go ahead."

The M.E. folded the sheet down to the collarbones. "Poor fella. This is what taking a gunshot to the face does to ya."

Kimber took a bracing breath before she looked down. Dear God. She'd been around a lot of corpses—with her job there was no way around it—but she'd never seen anything quite this bad. Bile rose in her throat. She swallowed it down and backed up a few steps.

Bishop's hand came out to steady her. "You okay?"

She nodded. She had a job to do, and the sooner she did it the sooner she could get out of there. "I'm fine." She moved forward and rested one hand on the corpse's shoulder. Her palm tingled. Good. Some vitality remained, which let her know this man had been dead only a couple of days at the most. If he'd been dead longer than that, well…With each day that passed after death, the energy dissipated more and more. Then it took a major blood sacrifice—a goat or several chickens—to reunite the soul with the body for even a few minutes. There was awesome power in pain and blood.

But with this poor guy, she could summon his soul by using a relatively small amount, so she'd use her own. Then they could find out who had put him in this state. "What's his name?" she asked.

The M.E. consulted the file in his hand. "Richard Whitcomb."

Kimber wondered who he'd been, what he'd planned to do with his life before someone took it from him. There wouldn't be time to find out. There would only be time to help him through his initial confusion and find out who killed him, if he even knew.

She withdrew the knife she kept sheathed at the small of her back. The hilt was a familiar, comforting weight in her hand. After broadening her stance, she sliced across her inner forearm, a long but not very deep cut, just below a faint row of thin scars. Even though the laceration was shallow, she sucked in her breath at the sharp sting. She walked a circle around the gurney, allowing a miniscule amount of her blood to drip on the floor. Once she'd completed her circuit, she stood inside the circle of power and let her blood drip onto the face of the dead man, making sure it covered his mouth before wiping the blade on the sheet. She slid the knife back into its scabbard. She'd make sure to sterilize it once she got home.

The M.E. handed her a gauze pad and a strip of medical tape. She secured the gauze over her wound and placed her palm on the shoulder of the corpse again. Called by the life essence in her blood, the mists of the netherworld—that shadowy place where all life began and ended—began to stir. So far, so good. Kimber started to chant. "Hear me, Richard Whitcomb. I call you from beyond. I call you to journey from the Unseen to the Seen. By blood and magic I summon you. Arise, Richard. Arise. Come to me now." She always made sure to use the singular when she summoned someone from the dead. She wanted to make sure she was the only one who controlled them. She'd seen firsthand how horrific a summoning could become when the dearly departed had been brought back by someone using "us" and "we" instead of "me" and "I."

She'd never make that mistake again.

The fine hairs on the back of her neck lifted. The magic of the Unseen rippled. The soul was almost reunited with the body. Just one more push should do it. "Richard, come to me. Arise, Richard. Arise!"

The palm of her hand tingled where it rested on his shoulder. He was reanimating. "Just a few more minutes," she murmured.

A surge of power flowed from the corpse up her arm, the energy of the Unseen coursing through her like an electrical charge, making her wince. What the hell? That wasn't normal. She could usually feel the Unseen but it had never reached for her like this before.

Though her instinctive reaction was to shake her hand, she kept it where it was. But she did take a step back, ready to break contact if she needed to, and thereby severing the conduit of her magic with that of the Unseen.

"Everything okay?" Bishop asked. He took a step closer to the gurney, hand on the gun at his waist, even though she knew that *he* knew bullets wouldn't stop this kind of zombie. Only the one who summoned him, through her magic and force of will, could compel an animated corpse to return to his eternal slumber. He could pump this guy full of bullets and as long as Kimber held sway over him, he'd keep right on coming. Headless, armless, legless, he'd keep on trying until the necromancer returned the essence that animated him to the Unseen.

"Yeah. Yes," she said more forcefully. She had a reputation to uphold. This was a little unusual, but nothing she couldn't handle. She'd been raising the dead ever since her power had manifested when she hit puberty. Almost twenty years now. Granted, eight of those years she'd been under the guidance of a mentor, but still, she had a lot of experience. More than most.

And right now she needed to bear down and put that experience to use. She focused her ability and drew on the Unseen. Another strong wave crashed into her but she maintained her contact with the dead man. "Richard Whitcomb, I summon you by blood and magic. Arise!"

A shudder worked its way through the corpse then pale lids flew open. Or, rather, a pale lid. The eye on the ruined side of his face was gone. Equally pallid lips parted on a groan. His one eye flicked back and forth. Frown lines creased his brow. When Kimber lightly squeezed his shoulder, his gaze skittered to her face.

"It's all right," she soothed. "Richard, you're safe. You can't be hurt anymore."

His mouth worked but no sound came out. His eye widened and he jerked against the metal table.

"Richard, it's all right," Kimber said again. She'd learned long ago that she needed to keep using the deceased's name; otherwise they took a much longer time remembering who they were and what they'd been doing right before they died. "Richard, look at me. Focus on me, Richard."

His head turned and that filmy blue eye fastened on her. His mouth continued to open and close; only now low, gruff grunts came out.

"It's all right," she whispered. "You're safe. Be calm." She felt some of the tension ease from the cold muscle beneath her palm. "That's it." She leaned closer. "Your name is Richard Whitcomb. Do you remember?"

He bobbed his head.

"Good." Kimber was aware on some level of the people around her, but she kept her attention on the dead man. He'd been human, once, maybe he still was, and that meant he deserved her respect. And some dignity. She grabbed the sheet just as it started to slide off to one side, and made sure his nudity remained hidden.

Confusion was still evident in his gaze. She needed to give him time to realize he was dead. Sometimes they got it right away. Sometimes it took a few minutes.

"Wh…where…"

When he didn't go on, she figured he wanted to know where he was. "You're at the County Medical Examiner's office."

His frown deepened. "H…how…"

She tightened her lips. He needed to remember how he got here, not have someone tell him. Otherwise he might not recall the details they were looking for.

"You were shot," the M.E. volunteered.

"Doc," she muttered. She looked at him and shook her head. This wasn't their first dance with the dead. He should know better.

"He seems confused. More than normal," he said. When she merely stared at him, he shrugged. "Sorry."

"Sh…shot?" Richard struggled to sit up. Kimber helped him. When the sheet slid to his waist she gave silent thanks that it kept the important bits covered up. She wasn't a prude, she'd seen naked man parts before, but she wasn't particularly thrilled about seeing them on a dead guy.

"What do you remember?" she asked him.

He gave a slight shake of his head and raised a trembling hand to his face. When he felt the ruin on the right side, he let out a cry.

"Richard, you're okay." Kimber gave another gentle squeeze to his shoulder. "Look at me." She repeated it until he turned his attention to her. "I won't let anyone hurt you again, all right?"

He swallowed. "All right." He looked down at his fingers and clenched them. "Feel…strange."

She couldn't even imagine how weird it was for him. She didn't pretend to know. "Tell me what you remember about that night." She glanced at the stenographer. The woman tipped her chin to acknowledge she was ready.

A low sigh, almost a moan, came from the zombie. "We fought. We were always fighting. I don't think we knew how to do anything else."

"Who's we, Richard?" Kimber asked.

The click-clack of the steno's keys sounded loud in the otherwise quiet room.

Kimber leaned closer to the zombie. "Who did you fight with?"

He looked up. His confusion and sadness twisted into anger. "She did this to me!" He swung his legs over the side of the gurney. "She killed me."

It wasn't out of the ordinary for a murdered person to be out-raged upon realizing what had happened. It also wasn't unusual for them to become physically agitated as a way to work off some of the mental and emotional anguish. Even so, Kimber wanted to keep him as calm as possible. A calm dead man was one who went back to being dead with little effort. "Richard, it's all right. She can't hurt you again."

His one eye held dark rage. "I know she can't hurt me any-more. But I sure as hell can fuck her up."

Bishop took another step forward. "Kimber…"

She waved him off, never taking her gaze off Whitcomb. "Richard, I need you to pay attention." When he ignored her, she lost the soothing tone and made her voice commanding. "Richard Whitcomb, look at me."

He looked at her. She saw something move in his gaze, some-thing that felt dark. Evil. Something she'd never seen or felt be-fore at a reanimation. She tried to ignore the sensation that nig-gled at the back of her mind, that feeling that something was really, really wrong. She had a job to do; she could manage this.

To re-establish her magical connection, she placed her hand on his shoulder. His skin was still ice cold and dry to the touch. "Richard, who did you fight with? Who shot you?"

"My unfaithful slut of a wife." His thin lips pulled back in a gruesome smile. He jumped down off the gurney.

She tried to ignore the flash of teeth through his ruined cheek as well as the dead man's junk. "We'll make sure she pays for her crime," she promised him. "Now, get back on the gurney and we'll let you rest."

He gave a slow shake of his head. "No. I don't want to rest.

And I don't need you to make sure of anything. Oh, no." His chuckle came from a dry throat. "I'll take care of her, don't you worry."

That response wasn't all that unusual, either. The need for revenge was a common theme among murder victims.

Kimber drew upon the Unseen and felt her magic surge within her. "Richard Whitcomb, I command you to lie down."

He stared at her. "No." With a grimace he reached up and gripped her hand. He removed it from his shoulder but held onto it. He looked down at their fingers then began tightening his hand. His head came up and he stared at her from his one eye, malevolent pleasure shining there despite the film of death.

She winced at his hold. "Richard, let go."

"Can you make me, necromancer?"

That was not his voice. Someone—or *something*—else spoke through him.

Bishop moved forward. As he reached for Whitcomb, the zombie released Kimber and pushed her into the detective. She and Bishop stumbled back. Richard headed for the door.

"Whoa, there!" The M.E. grabbed the zombie by one arm and yanked him to a stop. "You're not goin' anywhere but into the ground, my man."

Whitcomb snarled. He struggled against the doctor's hold, but the older, portly man clearly had some strength beneath the flab. The two security guards and Bishop jumped in, quickly manhandling the zombie onto the gurney. While they held him, the M.E. strapped him in with duct tape while the stenographer looked on.

Every once in a while the woman glanced at Kimber. Her eyes

showed her fear and distaste over the situation, as well as a certain amount of distrust. Kimber couldn't blame her—if she'd been at a reanimation and the zombie had run amok, she'd wonder about the necromancer's skills, too.

"Kimber, what the hell?" Bishop faced her, his expression making the craggy lines of his face more pronounced. Rioting emotions enhanced the blue in his usually smoky gray eyes. "What just happened?"

Whitcomb started shouting obscenities and struggling against his bonds of tape. Even though the security guards remained beside him, Kimber kept an eye on him while she answered the detective. "I honestly don't know. There's something more inside him than just his soul."

Whitcomb's single-eyed gaze slid to her. "Wouldn't you like to know what I am, necromancer?" His slow grin sent a shudder through her that she did her best to suppress. He must have seen something, though, because he chuckled. "Not as cool a cucumber as you'd like your friends to think you are, eh?"

"We have what we need," Bishop said. "Finish it."

"She can't!" Whitcomb's shrill laugh bounced off the walls. "Little bitch isn't powerful enough."

"Now, see here…" The M.E. moved closer. "You keep talking like that and I'll duct tape your mouth."

Whitcomb's eyebrows climbed. He looked from the older man to Kimber and back again. "You got it for her bad, don't you, doc? She is awfully juicy, I agree." His gaze shifted to Kimber again. "Bet you're a hot little slut in bed, aren't you, necromancer?" He looked at her breasts and then lingered on the juncture of her thighs. "Yeah, baby. That's one sweet pussy."

"That's it." The M.E. tore off a piece of tape and reached for the dead man's mouth.

Whitcomb lifted his head and sharp teeth snapped down onto the doctor's hand. The M.E. cried out and jerked his hand away to the sound of the zombie's maniacal laughter. Kimber saw the drip of blood before the doctor turned and hurried to the hand wash station.

Kimber put both hands on Whitcomb. Her palms tingled from the supernatural energy animating his body. It surged toward her like before. This time she was prepared and tamped it down with her own magic. She stared into his ruined face and intoned, "Richard Whitcomb, I consign you to the grave. Your soul is released once more to its everlasting journey."

He continued to struggle and curse, but there didn't seem to be as much strength behind his efforts as before.

"Go to your eternal rest, Richard." Kimber ignored the curses he flung her way. She focused all her energy on him and felt the tingling in her hands begin to decrease. It was working. She caught sight of the fresh blood tingeing his mouth and realized she could use that. "By blood and magic, I consign you to eternity."

The fight went out of him like the strings cut to a marionette. Kimber kept her hands on him a few seconds longer, just to be sure. Once she was certain there was no more magic flowing between them, she withdrew her hands and blew out a breath. Now that she was no longer a magical conduit, exhaustion dragged at her. All she wanted to do was go home and climb into bed. She knew, like always, she'd have nightmares after tapping into the

Unseen. She just hoped this time they weren't worse than normal.

She looked around the room, meeting the gaze of the other occupants. Forcing gaiety into her voice she said, "Phew! That was something, wasn't it?"

The stenographer stared at her with accusation in her eyes then without a word gathered up her machine and left. The two security guards glanced at each other and followed her out. That left Kimber alone with the M.E., Detective Bishop, and the newly re-deceased Richard Whitcomb.

"That was *not* normal." Bishop's troubled eyes searched hers. "What the hell was that?"

She lifted her hands. "I don't know." At his skeptical expression, she insisted, "Bishop, seriously. I have no idea. I've never had that happen before." She glanced at Whitcomb. "But it's over now, so all's right with the world. He told you who killed him, so…" She looked at Bishop again. "Go get 'er."

He shook his head, but she saw a smile tug at one corner of his mouth. He looked over at the M.E. "Doc? You okay?"

The doctor waved at him without turning around. "I'm fine, though it's the first time I've been bitten by one of my…patients."

It wasn't the first time a zombie had gone after someone like Whitcomb had the M.E., but it was certainly the first time she'd seen one take a bite out of anyone.

"Good. I'll see you later." Bishop looked down at Kimber. "You look tired. This one really took it out of you."

"I'll be all right." He was a nice guy, the real deal. Why she couldn't feel anything romantic for him was beyond her. But then, who had time for romance when there were the dead to raise and put back down? She sent him a smile. "Take care, Bishop."

"You, too. Time to go save the world." He gave her a jaunty two-fingered salute and sauntered out of the room.

Kimber walked over to the M.E. "Are you sure you're okay?" She placed one hand on his upper arm.

He finished taping the gauze wrapped around his hand and held it up. "I'm good to go," he said. He met her eyes. "This is my own damn fault for getting within biting distance. But, hell, girl, none of 'em's ever done that before."

She shook her head. "No, I've never seen it happen, either." And it had never been as hard to put one back to rest. She needed to talk to another necromancer, or maybe a few, and see if they'd ever experienced something like this. Or was she the lucky one?

She made sure Whitcomb was really still dead and said her good-byes to the doctor. She grabbed her handbag from the chair by the door and left the room. As she exited the building, she saw a man sitting on the trunk of her twenty-year-old POS that still ran in spite of being held together by hope and rusted bits of metal. The illumination from the pole light she'd parked under gave a glossy sheen to his black hair. When he saw her he slid to his feet.

Duncan MacDonnough. Vampire prince-wannabe and royal pain in her ass. She'd known him for a couple of years. There'd been an initial, immediate attraction she'd done nothing to fight until the night she'd realized what he was and what that meant for her—that because of him she and her parents had come to the attention of the local vampire queen, and her parents had died.

After that she'd made sure to keep things friendly but not too friendly, but there had always been a sexual undercurrent flowing between them she couldn't deny. She knew if she issued an invitation to her bed he'd take her up on it. She just wasn't overly interested in a relationship where her lover could drain her dry. No matter how sexy he was.

"Duncan," she greeted. After the night she'd had she was in no mood to put up with any of his crap.

"Kimber." His deep, husky voice rasped across her ears. As usual, his demeanor was solemn. Somber. "I hear you had some trouble tonight."

She stopped a few feet away from him and crossed her arms with a scowl. "And how did you hear that?"

"Bishop." He rested a lean hip against the back fender of her vehicle. It creaked and she had the hope it wouldn't fall off. How embarrassing would that be? Duncan added, "We talked briefly when he came out to his car."

She frowned. "What, you've just been hanging out in the parking lot?"

One of his dark brows quirked. On anyone else she would have thought it to be a sign of humor. With Duncan…She didn't think she'd seen him smile more than a handful of times over the years she'd known him. "As a matter of fact…I was not," he said. "I came to see the doc, but when Bishop told me what happened and said you were on your way out, I thought I'd wait to talk to you out here."

"Talk to me about what?"

"You know about what."

She tightened her lips. She was not going to work for him or his queen. There was nothing in the world that would make her join forces with a bunch of bloodsuckers, even if she did regularly spill her own blood on the job. For one, she didn't trust that none of them would bite her. Second, she didn't trust that none of them would bite her. Yeah, that whole biting thing they had going on was the overriding reason she refused to work for them.

She shoved memories of her parents' dying expressions, agonized and fearful, to the back of her mind. "There's nothing to talk about," she muttered and moved forward. "Get off my car."

He straightened and let her unlock the door. As she opened it he said, "Maddalene is very determined, Kimber. And very old, which means she's more powerful than you can know. I've never known her to not get what she wants eventually."

"Well, then, I guess she'll finally have to learn what disappointment feels like." She tossed her purse onto the passenger seat and turned to face Duncan. He was less than six inches away. She gasped and backed up until she bumped into the open car door. She hadn't heard him move. It was surprise that made her move back, that was all. It certainly wasn't because he was a hot, sexy beast that made her want to forget about all her misgivings. It had nothing to do with those clear glass-green eyes of his that seemed to see into her soul. Nothing to do with the way the muscles of his shoulders, arms and chest seemed to beckon her to rest within their shelter. Nothing to do with the way his night-black hair beckoned her fingers to twine in its depths.

He rested a long arm on the roof of her car and bent toward her, effectively caging her in the opening of her car. "Be careful. She won't put up with this attitude of yours any more than she'll continue to accept your refusal." His somber gaze held hers. "She wants your necromancy services, Kimber. She'll keep coming until you give in."

Kimber crossed her arms and tipped her head back so she could look into his handsome face. He had six inches on her in height and outweighed her by at least a hundred pounds, making her feel feminine. Protected, even though he was what he was.

She looked her fill. Pretty, pretty man with long black eyelashes framing those incredible eyes. Her gaze drifted to his mouth, those sensual lips that tempted her so much. She drew in a bracing breath. It would take more than what he had to make her put herself into harm's way. As much as she didn't want to, the memory of her parents' deaths at the hands of vampires—vampires who had been under Maddalene's command—that memory kept flashing into her thoughts. It didn't matter that Duncan had destroyed the ones who'd killed her parents. It was all too little too late. There was no way he would tempt her to forget exactly what he was, what he was capable of.

Yep, keep telling yourself that, Kimber. Maybe at some point it'll actually be true. She cleared her throat. "She can't force me."

"Can't she?" He leaned closer until his mouth was a mere inch from hers. "You have no idea what she's capable of."

"Oh, I think I do. I have a scar to prove it, remember? You were there."

"And you've never forgiven me for not protecting you then."

She clenched her teeth. He'd promised no harm would come to her, and she'd believed him. She'd trusted him. Even after Maddalene had given the order to have Kimber's parents used as vampire bait, Kimber had believed that Duncan would somehow protect her from the bitch queen. He'd kept Maddalene from killing her, but Kimber had a scar that ran from the left side of her throat down her back—a constant reminder of her fight with the vampire race.

"No, I haven't," she said in answer to his claim. In reality, she had, at least intellectually. Emotionally was another matter. It all came down to trust, and she wasn't sure she could trust him.

He was so close she could see herself reflected in his eyes. Her pulse pounded in her throat. She resisted the urge to clap her hand over it, though as close as he was she suspected he could hear the increased rhythm of her heart. She couldn't deny his appeal, and she refused to be ashamed of having a natural reaction of female to male. But she wasn't going to let him seduce her into doing something she didn't want to do. "I said no, and I meant no."

He stared into her eyes. She didn't feel him in her head, so she knew he wasn't trying to use his vampire wiles to influence her. "You need to reconsider," he said, his breath puffing against her lips as he spoke. "I promise you, this time I *will* protect you. With my life if need be." His voice deepened. "I'm telling you this for your own good, Kimber. Reconsider."

She planted her palms on his chest and pushed him back, aware with some anger that the only reason she was able to budge him was because he allowed it, not because she'd been strong enough. "Is that a threat?" she asked, staring hard at him. She didn't care if he was faster and stronger than she was. She wasn't going to let him intimidate her. She made sure her voice was hard and tough. "Are you threatening me?" She almost added "punk" to the end but her sense of self-preservation prevailed.

Nevertheless, his eyes narrowed at her tone. "No, I'm not. I'm trying to help you."

"Help…" She shook her head. Vampires didn't ordinarily go out of their way to help people, especially people like her, people who held sway over the dead. It made them nervous, she supposed, seeing as how they, too, had been dead once upon a time. They had to have the thought, somewhere in the back of their minds, that maybe, just maybe, she'd be able to control them if she put her mind, and her magic, to it. She hadn't ever seriously considered doing it, because if she tried and couldn't, it would be very bad for her. Or if she was successful and then released control—again, it would be very bad for her.

Tapping into the Unseen wasn't something she did on a whim. It took a lot out of her, and she nearly always ended up with nightmares for a few nights after. Most other necromancers she knew did, too. No one really knew why, though they assumed it was because of the power they drew upon to reanimate the dead.

In an effort to sort the mishmash that was her brain at the moment, she closed her eyes for a second. She couldn't think clearly and look into that gorgeous face. When she lifted her lids again it was in time to see his dark head bend close. Passion flared in his eyes before he hid it by dropping his lashes. Then his lips slanted over hers and she lost her breath. And maybe her mind because, God help her, she liked it. A lot.

This was the first time he'd followed through on the desire she'd seen reflected in his eyes from the first time they'd met. A reciprocated desire she kept trying to deny to herself. But now, with his kiss, the truth was impossible to refute. His mouth was cool against hers at first, quickly warming from contact with her lips.

Her eyelids fluttered shut and she leaned into him, wrapping her arms around his waist. Big hands came up and cupped her face, tilting her head to the angle he wanted as he devoured her lips. His tongue glided between her lips to tease and torment. He swallowed her low moan. One hand slid down to her waist, drawing her closer, while the other hand cradled her skull, fingers tangling in her hair.

Kimber slid her hands around to Duncan's back. Feeling off-balance, she gripped his shirt to hold on in a world gone topsy-turvy. The feel of his firm flesh beneath the fabric served to heighten the desire she'd denied earlier. Now it flared to new life, setting her heart to pound hard against her ribs and her core to soften.

He lifted his head and stared into her eyes. Whatever he saw there made him groan. His mouth crashed onto hers again, lips nibbling, rubbing. The hand at her waist moved lower, shaping her buttock, pulling her closer.

The hard evidence of his desire excited her even further. Moaning softly, she pressed against his erection and skimmed her hands up his chest to hold his head. Silky dark hair slid through her fingers.

His mouth left hers to travel along her jaw then down her neck. When his lips slid to the pulse point in her throat, she stiffened and pushed him away. God in heaven, what had she been thinking, letting him kiss her? Letting him get close enough to bite. But that was the problem, wasn't it? She *hadn't* been thinking.

"Kimber—"

"Don't." She held up one hand. "Just…don't." She was tired and felt like an idiot. Another second and she would've let him take her right there against her car. Take her with fangs and cock. She rolled her shoulders and stared at him, feeling like she was a hundred years old. "Anything for your queen, is that it, Duncan?"

He scowled. Apparently he didn't like her calling him a prostitute. Too bad. She didn't appreciate him trying to seduce her so she'd acquiesce to his queen's demands.

"I didn't kiss you because Maddalene wants you to work for her." His face lightened and he looked at her mouth. "I kissed you because I wanted to. Because I've been wanting to taste you, feel those courtesan lips of yours beneath mine."

Now who was calling whom a prostitute? "Did you just call me a whore?" She raised her eyebrows. When he appeared to be a bit discomfited and denied her charge, her good humor returned. She was never one to pass up an opportunity to give a vampire a hard time. "I'm certain that 'courtesan' is a pretty name for 'whore'. And if you think I have courtesan lips, then…" She tilted her head to one side and studied him, pointedly waiting for a response.

"I don't think you're a whore," he finally said. His tone was dry and his expression said *touché* as clearly as if he'd verbalized it. "I do, however, think you're a brat."

She couldn't hold back her grin. It felt good to finally get this composed, always in control man as off kilter as he got her. Even if it was only for a couple of seconds. "I'll see you later," she said and got into her car. She closed the door and cranked down the window. "You can tell your queen that my answer is still no."

As she drove away she glanced in her rearview mirror. Duncan was nowhere to be seen. Sneaky bastard. But what else could she expect? He was a vampire, and they were the definition of duplicitous. It was too bad, really. Now that she'd kissed him, she could definitely go back for more. If he weren't what he was.

For now they'd play this cat and mouse game and she'd see just how long she could hold out against Maddalene Vanderpool's demands.

Chapter Two

Six months later

Kimber stood in the small kitchen of her apartment and stared at the black plastic covering the window over the sink. It was easy to say her life had taken a turn for the worse over these last several months, but certainly not any worse than anyone else's. After that night with Whitcomb, the night when Duncan kissed her and made her think of things that could never be, the Chief Medical Examiner had fallen ill. The bite on his hand had appeared infected, dark lines shooting up his arm, his skin turning fiery red. But within forty-eight hours his temperature had broken, the infection had cleared, and he'd gone to a neighborhood block party...where he promptly went a little crazy and started attacking people. He had managed to bite a dozen people before he was restrained. He'd died three days later. But he hadn't remained dead.

His wife erupted at the gravesite service, cursing those around her and biting anyone who tried to help. A day later someone else who'd been bitten at the party, while traveling in Europe on business, began raving at business colleagues and bit anyone who got too close.

At first no one realized what was happening, and by the time anyone did, by the time the experts concluded that the world had a full-blown pandemic on their hands spreading through a bite, it was much too late.

Now the zombie apocalypse was in full swing. From the Chief Medical Examiner—Patient Zero—the Outbreak had happened, plunging the world into chaos. And everyone blamed Kimber for it. While the Internet had still worked she'd been the subject of too many memes and tweets to count. There had been hurtful, nasty messages left on her voice mail, scrawled on her car, her apartment building. So much so that she'd moved in with her assistant without anyone else being aware of it.

Maybe it *was* her fault, but she honestly didn't know what went wrong. She'd done her job that night the same way she had for years. The only conclusion she kept coming up with was there was something wrong in the Unseen. Or, rather, there *had* been something wrong there.

Now…now it was here.

"You're thinking dark thoughts again." Her friend and former assistant Natalie Lafontaine held out a coffee carafe.

Kimber held out her ceramic mug. Natalie poured it half full with coffee, tipped some of the dark brew into her own cup and replaced the blue speckled enamelware coffee pot on the one-burner camp stove sitting on the kitchen counter.

"I'm not thinking anything," Kimber murmured and took a small sip from her cup.

"Uh-huh. You get that look on your face every time you start thinking about the apocalypse. But I'm not going to tell you, for the thousandth time, it wasn't your fault." Without waiting for Kimber's response, Natalie went on. "Nothing like roughing it in the middle of the city," she said, keeping her voice low as they all had to do. The apartment was well-insulated but not soundproof. While the zombies' sense of smell wasn't the greatest, they had decent hearing. Loud noises caught their attention, so survivors of the Outbreak had learned to be quiet.

Natalie sighed and sat down in the chair next to Kimber. The small dining room in Kimber's apartment was dimly lit by two pillar candles in the center of the table. With black trash bags taped over the windows of the apartment, the area outside of the dining room was in complete darkness.

"We're going to need more propane for the camp stove soon. And that's the last of the coffee," Natalie murmured. She leaned an elbow on the glass top table and propped her chin in her hand. "Unless we beat up the old ladies in 315 for their stash."

Kimber snorted. "I don't think we're there just yet." She took a sip and stared into her cup. Only a few swallows left. She looked at Natalie. "Maybe tomorrow."

Natalie gave a bark of laughter. Her eyes widened and she slapped her hand over her mouth. "Sorry," she mumbled around her fingers.

Kimber went still, too, listening carefully, but didn't hear any movement from the hallway. There were several other survivors living in the building, a few on this floor, and most had settled into small groups of three or four in order to pool their resources. Some, though, stayed alone. She was pretty sure that the guy who lived at the end of the hall hadn't left his apartment since the Outbreak first hit the news. He could be dead for all she knew. She wasn't going to check up on him, because for one thing, she'd seen enough dead bodies and, for another, he could have wandered out and gotten bitten. She wasn't going to take a chance.

She and Natalie could be relatively certain they were secure here because they checked frequently to make sure none of the living dead made it into the safe harbors established inside this wing of the apartment building. But nothing was completely impregnable.

The bathroom door opened and their other roommate came down the hallway. Aodhán was dressed in jeans and a black T-shirt that showed off his muscled arms and torso. His damp hair evidenced his recent shower. His big feet were bare and soundless as he padded past them into the living room. Except for the threat of zombies outside and the fact that Aodhán was fey and held a sword in one hand, it seemed a normal tableau.

But she knew nothing was normal, not anymore. Not for the past six months. Food was scarcer, for one thing. And so far the water supply was holding out, but it was only a matter of time before the unattended infrastructure completely broke down. While she could survive without coffee—though she wasn't sure those around her would—no human being could live long without food and water.

Electricity was a thing of the past. They used candles indoors and, if they had to travel after dark, flashlights. Batteries weren't easy to come by, so they did their best not to be out at night. They had rope ladders at every window so that if they were overrun they could get out.

They kept warm with the wood burning stove they'd rigged up. They had multiple wood stacks in the vacant apartment next door. The venting ran up through the ceiling and into an unused apartment on the fourth floor. The windows were open there so the smoke had a place to escape. This past winter they'd all bedded down in the living room around the stove. In another month when spring moved into summer, they should be able to start using the bedrooms again.

And that was the other thing that had changed. The two-bedroom apartment where she used to live with Natalie now housed four people from time to time—two humans, one fey warrior and a vampire who was thankfully absent for the moment. With only half a cup of coffee she wasn't sure she'd be able to put up with bossy-pants Duncan MacDonnough.

Even if his bossiness made her want to roll over and do whatever he wanted.

She'd thought about suggesting they all get a place of their own. It wasn't as if there weren't plenty of empty apartments available. And she'd sure as hell thought plenty about telling Duncan to stay at his own place at Maddalene's complex. But while having people living with her was aggravating at times, she could still recognize that there was safety in numbers. If for no other reason, she and Natalie could sleep while Aodhán or Duncan kept watch, and vice versa.

From where he sat on the sofa, Aodhán said, "I know I don't need to remind you to keep your voices down." The lovely Irish lilt did nothing to mask the slight ring of condescension in his deep voice.

"No, you don't," Kimber muttered. She finished her coffee and placed the mug on the table. "Although it does sound quite lovely when you *don't* remind us."

He turned his head and looked at her. She only knew it because the light from the candles on the table glinted in his eyes.

"Oh, for crying out loud." She picked up one of the candles and carried it carefully into the living room. She set it on the coffee table and sat down on the other end of the sofa. "I can't even see you from in there." Curling her legs beneath her, she rested her head against the back of the sofa and stared at him. He picked up a soft cloth and stroked it along the sword blade. She frowned. "You cleaned that thing yesterday, and you haven't used it since."

"A sharp, clean sword is a warrior's best friend." He lifted a brow. "It also makes it much easier to lop off heads. Or, if you'd prefer, I can let it get dirty and dull and then hack away at the hordes when we face them. Take five minutes to do a job that should only take a few seconds."

"Are you sure that's it?" Natalie asked as she walked over to them. "Or do you just like fondling your sword?"

Kimber pressed her lips together, her gaze going from Natalie to Aodhán. These two had struck sparks from the moment they'd met, and it had only gotten worse with their close living quarters. She wasn't sure if she should fix some popcorn or take cover.

"Oh, I'm like any other man, lass," he rejoined with a smirk. "I'm not averse to fondling my mighty sword. Of course, I'm also highly inclined to allow those of the feminine persuasion the opportunity to wrap their hands around it, to stroke along the hard shaft all the way to the tip." He gave a lecherous waggle of his brows.

Natalie rolled her eyes and shook her head. Kimber snorted back a laugh.

Without taking his gaze off Natalie, he asked, "Do you have something against fondling a man's sword, then?" He stretched his long legs out under the coffee table.

"I like fondling plenty. With the right weapon," Natalie added without missing a beat. "But that's something you'll only find out in your dreams, fairy boy."

Rather than be incensed by her derogatory name calling, Aodhán grinned, his teeth flashing white in the dim room.

Natalie propped her hands on her hips, clearly done with the conversation. "Are you finished in the bathroom?"

"Aye."

She looked at Kimber. "I'm going to take a shower. Assuming he and his mighty sword left some hot water." Without waiting for a response, she stalked down the hallway.

Kimber waited until the door closed behind her friend before she said, "You know, you shouldn't tease her like that. Things are difficult enough as it is."

"She started it." When she opened her mouth to reply he held up one hand and forestalled her. "I know, I sound like a wee lad in knee britches, don't I? I'm sorry. I'll do better. At least," he flashed another charming grin, "I'll try."

Kimber gave him a slight smile. She wished things were different and she could let these two people snipe at each other without curtailment. It was their way of flirting, she figured. But life was short, and dangerous, and the last thing any of them needed was for Natalie or Aodhán to be carrying on like that when zombies came.

She stared down at her hands. Life had gotten complicated but at the same time it was so simple. Complicated because there was a full-fledged zombie apocalypse going on and many people, most people, thought it was her fault.

She thought it was her fault.

But life was simple because there was no room to be concerned about possessions or wealth or fame. Life consisted of worrying about where the next meal was coming from, wondering whether there would be enough water, hoping they'd be able to find more propane for the cooking equipment and gasoline for the generator that powered the water heater, planning the garden they'd plant come summer, and fearing that zombies would get inside the safe zones of the building and break down their door. The anxiety was endless.

One on one she could defeat any zombie that came at her. But the living dead's strength was in their numbers. At some point even the strongest fighter could simply be overwhelmed by a horde.

And it wasn't as if they had anywhere else to go. One of the last news broadcasts before TV and radio stations went dark revealed the infection, or whatever it was, had spread worldwide.

"What are you thinking?" Aodhán set his sword on the table and rested one brawny forearm along the back of the couch.

She pinched the bridge of her nose and blew out a breath. "What I'm always thinking about," she whispered. "Them. And that it's all my fault."

"Do I have to tell you again what I've been telling you for six months, *mo chara*?" He leaned toward her and took her hands in his. His callused palms were warm against her skin. Aodhán had become her confidant, in spite of the fact he was buddies with a certain irritating vampire, and had taken to calling her "little friend" in his lovely lilting Irish Gaelic. Usually it served as a balm to her battered nerves. But tonight…not so much.

She didn't need him to repeat the meaningless words. "No, because it *didn't* happen to another necromancer, Aodhán," she said. "It happened to *me*." She pulled her hands away from his and stood up. She started to pace. "And I should've known…"

When she didn't go on, he prompted, "You should have known what?"

She pressed her lips together and plopped sideways into the oversized recliner, letting her legs dangle over the padded arm. "There was something different about the Unseen that night. It seemed to…*reach* for me." She met his bright blue eyes. "It's never done that before. Maybe if I'd stopped, if I'd aborted the ritual…" She huffed a sigh and shook her head. "I dunno. I should've done *anything* different than what I did, which was just plow right ahead because I had a job to do. A reputation to maintain."

He rested his ankle across the opposite knee and stretched both arms along the back of the sofa. "Hindsight is always the clearest. You had no way of knowing what would happen." He leaned forward, his gaze somber. "And all the coulda-shoulda-wouldas in the world won't change what happened."

A smile caught her by surprise. She hadn't felt like smiling in…forever, it seemed.

"What's so funny?" he asked.

She shook her head. "You are." When he frowned, she held up one hand, palm up. "I just mean you're centuries old, you're a warrior—with a mighty sword, for crying out loud—and to hear you say 'coulda-shoulda-woulda' struck my funny bone. That's all."

"You know I'm right."

"Knowing," she said with a finger tapping her forehead, "and *knowing*," she went on with two fingers over her heart, "are two different things."

"Can't argue with you on that one." He reached for his sword and the sharpening stone he always left on the end table.

The key turned in the front door. Kimber and Aodhán both jumped up, he with his sword gripped tight in his right hand, instantly ready for battle.

Duncan walked in. He closed and locked the door behind him and quirked a brow at them. "You think zombies are going to have a key?"

"Shut up." Aodhán sat back down and started sharpening his sword.

"Kimber," Duncan said in greeting. He walked over and dropped down onto the end of the sofa. His dark hair was mussed, slight curls flopping onto his forehead. A tire iron hung from his belt loop.

Whatever the infection was that turned humans into zombies, it didn't work on vampires, at least not from the aspect of turning them into shuffling undead. But it was just as deadly to vampires as it was to humankind, causing the infected vamp to die a horrible and agonizing true death. So they couldn't use their teeth as a weapon like they would under other circumstances. They'd had to improvise, just like everyone else.

She glanced at Aodhán. He'd been pretty close-mouthed about whether the fey could get infected. She had a feeling they could, or maybe they didn't know yet. When the Outbreak happened, most fey returned to their own realm, refusing entry to anyone not fey, leaving humans to deal with the problem or be overtaken by it.

At least vampires hadn't completely abandoned them. Of course, that was probably because humans were their preferred food source. She turned her attention to Duncan and tried to ignore how delicious *he* looked. And realized that since he was here it meant it was dark outside. Already? *Damn it.*

"I hate this." Kimber folded her arms across her chest. "Damned windows all taped up. We don't know what freaking time it is anymore. We only know that it's dark because you show up." Her voice cracked. She cupped her hands around her elbows, not sure how much more of this she could take. It felt like the least little thing would shatter her beyond repair. She needed a good scream. Which she couldn't have.

The next best thing would be a good cry. Which she wouldn't do, especially in front of Duncan. She didn't want him thinking she was weak. And immediately she grew irritated at herself for caring one way or the other what he thought. She didn't base her choices on what Duncan would think. This wasn't a What-Would-Duncan-Do world. She let loose a growl of frustration.

"Easy," Duncan murmured.

She took a deep breath and held it several seconds. "I'm all right," she finally said. She sat back down and looked at him. "Did you have any trouble getting here?"

He shook his head. "The area's quiet. For the moment. We must be in between waves."

Waves of zombies. Hordes. Herds. Gaggles. She stared at their blacked-out windows. She'd heard the living dead referred to in all of those ways, first in graphic novels, never really dreaming one day they would be a reality.

Well, reality sucked.

* * *

Duncan caught Aodhán's eye and jerked his head toward the bedrooms. His friend gave a slight nod and stood. "I think I'll go have a lie down." He gathered up his sword and walked down the hallway.

"It's kinda early, isn't it?" Kimber called out as the bedroom door closed behind him. "Of course, since I have no freaking idea what time it is, it could be after midnight for all I know," she muttered. She looked at Duncan and narrowed her eyes. "You told him to leave the room, didn't you?"

"You've been sitting right there. I didn't tell him to do anything."

"You did some kind of guy thing," she said in a low, taut voice. She was strung tight. They all were. Death haunted every corner and, for her and Natalie especially, with food in short supply, the misty shroud lurked within these walls of safety.

He wasn't going to play games with her, not now. "I needed to talk to you in private so, yes. I motioned for him to make himself scarce." He paused, trying to find the right words to once again broach this particular topic.

"You plan to talk to me tonight? Or maybe some time next week?"

He shot her a frown. She sassed him at every turn. When

they'd first met, it had irritated the hell out of him. Truth be told, it still did, but now he usually felt an undertone of humor bobbing below the irritation. But he wasn't going to let her see that. She'd feel like she'd got one up on him. "I want you and Natalie to move in with me. You'll be safer at my place than here in the middle of Zombie Central."

Kimber's eyes went wide. "You think we'll be safer surrounded by vampires?" She gave a decidedly unfeminine sounding snort. "It's not like you live in a house in a gated community, Duncan. You live in Maddalene's enclave on the edge of downtown. In a bunch of old reclaimed rubber factory buildings. With lots of other vampires." She must have added that last part because she thought he was slow and hadn't gotten her point the first time she'd made it.

"I give you my word you wouldn't be harmed." He leaned forward, clasping his hands between his knees. "Just how much longer do you think you can survive here? Each time we go out in search of supplies we have to go farther and farther afield. One of these times we might not be able to make it back."

"Listen, I never asked you to be my protector. If you're not happy with my living situation, there's the door." She stood and walked over to the wood burning stove. April in northeast Ohio meant it was still cold once night fell. Though he wasn't sure she had moved to the stove in order to keep warm. Since she was clothed in sweatpants, hooded sweatshirt and thick socks, he had a feeling her real motivation was to put distance between them. With her back to him she said, "Make sure to leave your key."

Duncan sat back and forced himself to stay where he was even though he was tempted to go over and try to shake some sense into her. Or kiss her senseless. Or both. Their one and only kiss had happened six months ago. Sometimes he thought she wanted him; sometimes he was sure of it, but most of the time he kept his distance because she clearly wasn't ready to pursue a relationship with him. He was patient. He could wait. He'd gotten a taste of her mouth and wanted more. Much more. She was the only one who made him feel like a human again. Not a monster…and he'd done some monstrous things in the last eighty years. Even before he'd become a vampire he hadn't been a good man. But in Kimber he saw a chance for redemption. So he'd wait as long as he needed to. In a low voice he said, "If I hadn't decided to protect you and gotten Aodhán to help, just how long do you think you and Natalie would have lasted?"

She whirled to face him. The light of the lone candle on the coffee table threw her face into an interesting mix of lights and shadows, but with his excellent night vision he had no difficulty seeing the expression in her eyes. She was angry, frustrated, and scared. And she was taking it out on him. He was fine with that. He wanted to keep Kimber safe. Beyond that, he had a favor he wanted to ask of her, a big one. But he had to wait for the right time.

"I'm no slouch when it comes to self-defense," she muttered. She pointed a slender finger at him. "I carried a dagger for my job, remember?"

"A dagger that you used to draw blood for your resurrection ritual, not for defense," he pointed out. "Six months ago you wouldn't have made it past the first horde."

Her lips tightened. She didn't say anything for a few moments. "You might be right," she responded quietly. She blinked. "I don't

think I've done anything except give you a hard time about it."
She sighed and dropped back into the recliner.

He hated to see that some of the fight seemed to have left her.
He'd much rather have her feisty than defeated.

"I should have said this a long time ago—thank you." She
crossed her arms. "Having said that, I'm not leaving Zombie Central to move into Vampire City. At least with zombies I can run
to get away from them."

"Not if you're surrounded," he muttered. "Kimber, I don't
think you—"

"Just stop, please. It's not only that your commune buddies
would like to sink their fangs into me. It's also that there are so
many of them." She gestured toward the back of the apartment. "I
lived alone, before the Outbreak. Now I have at least two, sometimes three people around me all the time. I can't go anywhere
to get some alone time and still feel relatively safe, except for the
bathroom, and it's freezing in there right now, so spending more
time in the bathroom than necessary really isn't an option." She
picked at the arm of the chair. "It's making me crazy. Moving in
with you would exacerbate that tenfold."

Duncan could understand her desire for solitude. He preferred being alone most of the time, and his quarters allowed
that. "The difference is that I have three bedrooms, a den, a private walled-in patio, and twenty-four-seven security that patrols
the grounds to make sure no zombies get into the compound."
He saw a slight wavering in her eyes and pressed his advantage.
"You could have your own bed. Your own room." Never mind
that he'd prefer she share his bed. For now he wanted to get her
where she'd be safe. At least, saf*er*.

None of the vampires at the enclave would dare cross him, not if they wanted to continue to exist. As Maddalene's second in command, he had nearly as much authority as she did. In many matters he did have as much authority as she. No one doubted he was the alpha dog. A few had challenged him over the years, but he'd put them down.

He leaned forward. "What you need to remember is this: you're important to Maddalene. The last thing she wants is for you to come to harm. Anyone who touches you wouldn't live past dawn."

She pursed her lips. "That's great, Duncan. But I'd be dead, too, wouldn't I? So it's hardly a comfort to know that my killer would pay with his life. I'd rather know that some sort of preventive measures are in place." She stared at him. "Are there any?"

He scowled. "Short of wrapping you up in chain mail…no. There aren't." While he recognized that she had a point, it was galling that she wouldn't trust him to take care of her. Galling and…hurtful. That surprised him. He didn't want to look at the emotion too closely, so he pushed it to the side.

"Then I'm not moving in with you."

He heard the bathroom door open, and Natalie walked down the hallway, dressed in a floor-length flannel robe, rubbing a towel on her hair. "Just so you know," she said with a glance at Kimber, "there's no more hot water. Hey, Duncan," she added, looking at him. "How are you?"

She at least seemed happy to see him.

"I'm fine, thanks." He motioned toward Kimber. "Just trying to get your roommate here to see reason." He wasn't above using her friend against her if it advanced his position.

"Still trying to get us to move into the viper pit, huh?" Natalie stood with her back to the stove.

"Yes, he is," Kimber said. "And I've already told him no thanks."

"Hmm. Well, for what it's worth, I agree with you. Sorry, Duncan." She walked past the dining room, tossing the damp towel on the back of one of the chairs on her way to the small kitchen. "I'm going to start on dinner, such as it is." She paused and looked at Kimber. "I'm going to need to light a couple more candles so I can see what the hell I'm doing, all right?"

"Sure. You want some help?"

"No, I'm good."

Kimber watched Natalie putter around in the kitchen for a few seconds before she turned her attention back to Duncan. She pulled her feet up and sat cross-legged, hunching over with her elbows on her knees. Looking at Duncan, she muttered, "Anyway, going back to what we were talking about, I don't get why you care so much."

It was a question she'd asked him several times over the last six months. He'd dodged it each time. How could he tell her that he needed her to make contact with the Unseen? That he was desperate for a spiritual connection of some kind, any kind, so he could feel alive again? Feel human again. For her, or anyone else for that matter, to know that about him would paint him as weak. And he couldn't have that.

It was better for him that everyone assumed he had the hots for Kimber. And that conclusion wasn't too far from the truth. It just wasn't all of the truth.

The truth was, she was his second chance at life. To be a better man. And he was going to take that chance.

Chapter Three

I've told you. You're important to Maddalene." Duncan stretched his legs out in front of him.

Kimber studied him. "And she's important to you," she finally murmured.

"She is." He slouched down until he could rest his head against the back of the sofa and still be able to see her. "She saved my life. A couple of times."

"You've never told me this." She leaned forward and draped her hands over her ankles. "What happened?"

He clasped his hands across his belly and thought back over his past. He wouldn't tell her the whole story, because there was too much of it that was unsavory. He hadn't been a very good man when he'd been human, and the first few decades of his life as a vampire hadn't done anything to improve his character. He wasn't going to share what he was ashamed of. That shit needed to stay buried in his memories.

"I'm originally from Chicago; did you know that?" At the shake of her head, he went on. "I grew up on the north side, in a predominantly Irish neighborhood. The area had the highest crime rate in the city. Not joining a gang wasn't an option for boys, especially if you were Irish." He paused to gather his thoughts.

"So you were part of a gang?"

Duncan gave a one-shouldered shrug. "Part of the mob, actually. One of my best friends was Dean O'Banion. We started out as sluggers for the *Tribune*, then later the *Examiner*."

"I'm sorry, sluggers?"

"Hired thugs who beat up newspaper vendors who didn't sell our newspaper." It wasn't something he was proud of, but it had happened. By way of explanation he said, "Chicago before 1910 was rough, and it only got worse with Prohibition."

"I see." Kimber's tone was noncommittal, giving away nothing of what she felt. "Go on, please."

"Our little group of thugs became known as the North Side Mob, and as Prohibition continued, we were direct rivals of The Outfit, Al Capone's gang."

Her eyes widened. "You were part of all that?" She blew out a quiet whistle from between pursed lips. "I had no idea. Is that when you met Maddalene?" A wide grin broke out on her face. "She was a gangster's moll, wasn't she?" She gave a quick nod and tapped a finger against her chin. "I bet she was a gangster's moll. She probably went by the moniker Maddy the Moll. Or Long Maddy. Or Mad Maddy. Any of those would've worked, though I think maybe Mad Maddy is the best one. It's the truest descriptor."

"She wasn't a gangster's moll." He shook his head at her silliness. "Do you want to hear my story, or would you rather keep ragging on Maddalene?"

"I can do both," she responded with a smirk. "I'm an excellent multi-tasker."

Duncan scrubbed a hand over his chin.

"Okay, okay, I recognize that sign. Go ahead with your story. I'll try to behave."

He sincerely doubted that was possible. "Capone had Dean murdered in 1924. A few years later Bugs Moran became the leader." He paused and stared at his hands. He'd never particularly liked Moran. O'Banion had been tough, even cruel, but in those days that was what was needed. Weiss had been just as tough. Moran, on the other hand, had been cruel not out of necessity but out of desire. He'd thrived on the misery he could bring to others, especially Capone.

"I won't lie," he went on in a low voice. "They were horrible years, full of violence and infighting within the North Side Mob, and the killings of gang members on both sides." Unfortunately there had been a never-ending supply of local recruits—young men looking for fortune or fame or power. If that fateful day in February hadn't happened, if public sentiment hadn't turned against Capone, things in Chicago would probably have gotten a hell of a lot bloodier.

Duncan heard Natalie still moving about the kitchen, and the apartment was beginning to smell like hot dogs so dinner, such as it was, was well underway. He glanced over his shoulder to see her staring at him. Even though he and Kimber were keeping their voices quiet, the place was small enough that Natalie could hear what they were saying. That was all right. She had a right to know about him, too.

He turned back and looked at Kimber. "You ever hear about the Saint Valentine's Day massacre?" He waited for Kimber's nod before he continued. "Valentine's Day, 1929. Capone called for a truce. Another one." Duncan spread his hands. "We were always operating under truces that were always being broken, usually by Moran." He clasped his hands over his belly again. "Capone called for a meeting. There was about four inches of snow on the ground that day." He gave a low chuckle. "I remember how cold my feet were, and I was cursing Capone and his damned Outfit for dragging us out into it. So much so that I'd delayed leaving my apartment." He shook his head. "Just as I turned the corner, I saw a cop car behind the warehouse. I figured it was a raid, so I kept on going."

"But the cops were really Capone's men. I remember that from my American history classes." Kimber's mouth formed a small O. "Oh my God. You…you could've been killed."

Duncan grimaced. "If I hadn't been running late, I would have been inside the building when Capone's boys came in. So would Moran."

"Is that…" Her slender throat moved with her swallow. "Is that when Maddalene found you?"

"Several months later," he said. "Capone hadn't quite given up on the idea of making Moran a dead man. He just figured he'd have to be sneakier about it. People were tired of dodging bullets from Tommy guns," he said in a dry tone.

"Yeah, I imagine so."

"So Moran put together a plan to take care of Capone." He sat up straight, clasping his hands between his knees, and stared at his fingers. "Three of us went to a restaurant Capone was known to frequent. Things didn't go as planned." He glanced up at her. "I managed to get away, but I was wounded. Badly. I made it about two blocks before I collapsed."

Sympathy swirled in her eyes. She leaned forward, her fingers twisting in her lap. He wondered at the emotions he sensed from her. Would she have been sorry to hear some man she'd never met had died in a back alley long before she'd been born? Before even her grandparents had taken their first breaths?

Her lips parted. "Duncan. My God."

He grimaced. "I was praying, I can assure you. God answered my prayers in a way I never saw coming."

Kimber frowned then bit out a curse. "That's when Maddalene found you."

He gave a nod. "It was Black Monday. October 28th, 1929. If I'd died in that alley, it would have been a fitting end to a life that hadn't been well lived." As Natalie walked into the room, carrying two plates, he paused.

She handed Kimber a plate with a hot dog and a spoonful of beans then sat down on the other end of the sofa with her own plate in her hand. "I always feel strange, eating in front of you without offering you anything." She held out her plate. "Do you want some?"

"He doesn't eat food, Nat." Kimber picked up the hot dog. She brought it to her mouth and her tongue came out to lick a drop of juice at the end.

Duncan bit back a groan. There was another piece of meat he'd like to see her do that to. He shifted in his seat.

She took a bite and closed her eyes on a moan. When she swallowed the bit of hot dog she opened her eyes. "God, this tastes really good. There's nothing quite like a zombie apocalypse to make you appreciate the simple things."

Natalie let out a sigh and looked at Duncan. "It just feels weird, eating in front of you."

"Don't worry about it," Duncan assured her. "I'll…grab a bite later."

Kimber narrowed her eyes.

He rarely joked, and when he did she never seemed to appreciate his efforts.

"Don't even think about getting a bite here, buddy. I'll bust your balls."

"I'd like for you to try," he responded in a low voice. He was stronger and faster than she was, and his reach was longer. He'd have her flat on her back unable to do anything but plead for mercy. Which he might or might not give. He wanted another taste of that luscious mouth, wanted to trail his lips and tongue all over her body. Maybe even turn her luscious ass red with his hand before taking her from behind. His cock stirred against his thigh. He grimaced and shifted position again. "Where was I?" he asked. "Oh, yes. I was in that alley, lying amid trash and dirt, and I looked up to see the most beautiful creature I'd ever laid eyes on."

Kimber snorted. "Sorry," she muttered at his sharp look. "I don't disagree that physically she's beautiful. What's on the inside kinda ruins it for me, though. She had her vampires corner my parents like rats. They never had a chance."

He couldn't disagree with her, but she didn't know Maddalene the way he did. Like O'Banion back in the day, there was a reason for her cruel nature. "She found me in that alley and she turned me. She saved my life that day."

"She made you a vampire." Kimber shook her head. "I'm sorry, but I just don't see how that's a good thing."

He raised his eyebrows. "You and I would never have met, if she hadn't. I'd have been moldering in my grave these past eighty-four years."

Her expression went from startled to sad to one that suggested she didn't think that would have been a bad thing. When he frowned, she pressed her lips together but then a big grin broke out. "I'm sorry, but the look on your face…" She laughed, but stifled it quickly.

Natalie spoke up. "*I'm* glad you're here, Duncan."

"Thank you, Natalie." He shot a pointed look Kimber's way.

She giggled a few more seconds then got herself under control. "Really, I kid. As much as you irritate the hell out of me most of the time, I don't regret that we know each other."

She apparently didn't wish his permanent address was a cemetery, so at least there was that.

She shifted her position, crossing her legs, and began swinging one sock-clad foot in the air. "You said Maddalene saved your life a couple of times."

"Yes. The second time…" A knock sounded on the door. He stood, frowning when both Kimber and Natalie jumped up, their bodies tense. As Aodhán came out of the bedroom, sword in hand, Duncan's scowl deepened. "So now you think they'll knock on the door?"

"It could be someone looking to steal our food, smartass," Kimber muttered.

"Or they might want to rape us," Natalie added, her tone much more serious than Kimber's had been.

Duncan knew their fears were very realistic. Some men had taken advantage of the breakdown of society to allow their true natures out. He flashed his fangs. "I doubt a rapist would be polite enough to knock. Regardless, they'll have to get through me first."

"And me." Aodhán stood to one side of the door and gave Duncan a nod.

Between the lingering smell of hot dogs and the ever-present though faint smell of decomposition from zombies that always permeated the air—too faint for most humans to detect but more than enough for a vampire—Duncan couldn't get a good enough scent of whoever it was on the other side of the door. With a smooth motion, he twisted the lock and swung open the door. One of Maddalene's runners stood there—a pale, thin vampire, hand fisted to knock again. When he saw Duncan he lowered his arm. "Maddalene wants you," he said.

Duncan glanced at Aodhán and jerked his head toward the living room. Aodhán lifted his chin in acknowledgment and joined the women.

"Yeah, that's right. That's the place for him, hiding with the other girls," the vampire said, a sneer curling his upper lip away from his fangs.

Aodhán lifted his sword and took a step forward. "If you think you have what it takes, bring it on, little man."

"Boys, boys." Duncan lifted a hand to forestall Aodhán and looked at their visitor, who stood all of five and a half feet tall and if he was lucky weighed one thirty. Duncan leaned in close.

"Murray, do you really think you could take *him*?" He lifted an eyebrow. "Because I think Kimber could wipe the floor with you. What do you think an enraged fey warrior could do? And how fast do you think he could do it?"

Duncan knew the little vampire was stronger than Kimber; he'd merely said what he had to put the little bugger in his place. But Aodhán, on the other hand...Oh, hell yeah. Aodhán would have no problem getting the best of the vamp. Murray was small and wiry, and fast, which was why Maddalene used him as a runner. He could easily dart around zombies without getting caught. Unless he somehow got trapped in the middle of a horde. Then a lone vampire was SOL, no matter how fast he might be. The sheer weight of numbers trumped speed any day.

Murray's gaze darted to Aodhán, who stood at the ready, his long sword clutched in a white-knuckled hand. The vampire looked at Duncan. "I need to talk to you. In private."

"I'll be right back," Duncan told his friends without turning around. He joined Murray in the hallway, closing the apartment door behind him. "What do you want?"

"Not me. Maddalene. She wants you back at the complex. And she wants you to bring the necromancer."

Duncan folded his arms over his chest. Was Maddalene starting up her shit again? "Why?"

Murray shrugged. "She didn't say. I didn't ask. I like having my head attached to my body, thank you very much."

Duncan scowled. He'd been trying to get Kimber to move in with him so he could keep her safer than where she was at present. And he believed he *could* protect her, despite the fact she'd be also living with his queen.

Maddalene hadn't mentioned Kimber in a couple of months. He'd thought she'd backed down on wanting Kimber's services. But why else would she want the necromancer?

"Oh, and she said to make sure the fairy stayed behind. She doesn't want him tainting her surroundings." Murray gave a little smirk and then flicked two fingers in a salute. "You'd better shake your booty. You know she doesn't like to be kept waiting." Without waiting for a response, he walked down the hallway.

Duncan watched him leave. Only after the other vampire turned the corner did he go back inside Kimber's apartment.

The three were in the same positions he'd left them in. Upon seeing that Duncan was alone, Aodhán sheathed his sword and leaned one hip against the side of the sofa. "And just what was that about?"

"Maddalene demands my presence." Duncan looked at Kimber. "And yours."

Her brows shot up. "What? I don't think so. She's not *my* queen."

"Kimber." Duncan scrubbed his hand over his chin. "If you don't come with me now, she'll send someone else for you. Someone a lot scarier than me."

She propped her hands on her hips. "What does Her Majesty want?"

"I don't know." Duncan lifted one hand. "It's immaterial."

Kimber took a couple of steps toward him. "It's immaterial? The local queen of the vampires summons me, and you say the reason is *immaterial*?"

"Kimber." He couldn't keep the exasperation out of his voice. Damn it all, did she have to fight him on everything? He took her arm and drew her to the side of the room. Keeping his voice low, he said, "Remember what happened the last time you didn't do what she wanted?" To be fair, Maddalene hadn't intended to injure Kimber, but sometimes what a vampire means to be a firm touch is enough to hurt a more fragile human.

Her lips thinned. One hand cupped her shoulder. The dislocated joint was long healed, but he knew she remembered the incident clearly. "And yet you say you can keep me safe if I move in with you?"

"Yes. Yes, I can, because Maddalene respects my wishes. And she needs me, so she won't want to piss me off." He was ninety-nine percent sure that last part was true. Well, maybe ninety-eight. Or seven. Regardless, if he gave them sanctuary, he would die before he let harm come to her or her friends. "We need to go. Now."

She heaved a sigh. "Fine. I'll go see what she wants. But if I get eaten by Maddalene, I'm going to haunt you." She walked away from him. "Come on, Nat. Let's get our weapons."

The two women left the room, and Aodhán tipped his head to one side, studying Duncan. Finally the fey warrior said, "Are you sure you want to do this?"

He could read Duncan well and probably had picked up on micro-expressions on his face when he'd thought about how far Maddalene would let him go before she'd jerk back on the reins.

"There's not really an alternative," Duncan responded. "Unless we leave the city. Well, the state. But I gave my word to Maddalene that I'd stay as long as she need—"

"Screw that," Aodhán muttered. He straightened. "You've repaid your debt to her tenfold. She's taking advantage of your integrity, and you know it."

Before Duncan could respond, Kimber and Natalie rejoined them. Each woman held a flashlight in one hand and their weapons—a hatchet for Kimber and a short sword for Natalie—in the other hand. "We're ready," Kimber said. "Well, as ready as we'll ever be."

Natalie had a look of false anticipation on her face. "It'll be a grand adventure. I'm looking forward to it."

Duncan shook his head. Women. Couldn't live with them, couldn't feed them to hungry vampires.

Thoughts of him sinking his fangs into Kimber's throat, feeling her naked body beneath his as he also sank his cock into her hot depths, caused his body to tighten. With a muttered oath he opened the door and took a step back to avoid the fist coming down. His curse this time was louder. He hadn't even heard the man in the hallway. He had to keep his libido under control or he'd get them all killed.

Carson Bishop dropped his hand to his side. "Sorry," he said. "I was just getting ready to knock."

Duncan knew the ex-cop lived a few apartments down with a couple of his former colleagues. Close enough to Kimber to drop by any time he wanted. And he did. A flare of jealousy surged, one which made no sense, and Duncan tightened his mouth. The damned woman was making him crazy. "We're on our way out."

Bishop moved out of the way. "Where're you headed?"

"Maddalene's." Kimber raised her eyebrows and pulled a face. "The queen doth command our presence forthwith."

"Not mine, I'm sure," Aodhán interjected. "I'll go with you as far as MLK Drive, but I'm going to head north from there and check on my people."

"She specifically sent word that you were *not* to come," Duncan said.

"Fine by me."

Duncan looked at Bishop. "What brings you by?"

"I smelled hot dogs." He glanced at Kimber. "And if you're taking her to Maddalene, I think I'd better go along. Safety in numbers and all that."

"You think I'd allow harm to come to her?" Duncan stared at the former cop. Jealousy and anger tightened his gut, made his eyes burn.

"I think you'd fight until you can't fight anymore," came the quiet rejoinder. "But one more watching over her can't hurt, right?"

"She's standing right here, you know." Kimber's exasperation came through loud and clear. "Men."

"You're welcome to join us," Duncan said to Bishop. The man was a good fighter, and as he said, having another person to watch out for Kimber wouldn't hurt. Duncan didn't plan on letting her out of his sight, but another set of eyes with a warrior heart was welcome. "What about your friends?"

"Dave's down with a cold, the big wuss, and Mark and Henry are out on patrol." Bishop lifted his brows. "I can get them back by radio. You want them to come, too?"

Duncan shook his head. "One more is fine, three more turns us into a goddamned parade." He started down the hallway then led the way down the stairs. They made it out of the apartment complex without difficulty—the heavy duty wire fencing the residents had put up around the building was holding the zombies at bay. Right now there weren't any lingering around, which was good. But he didn't let himself think that they'd be that lucky the rest of the way. The moon was up, not quite full, but bright enough to light their way. They wouldn't have to use their flashlights.

Maddalene's compound was only a mile and a half to the southwest, but it might as well have been a hundred miles away since they had to dodge zombies to get there. "Stay close," Duncan murmured. He pulled his tire iron from the loop on his belt and gripped it in his left hand.

Duncan could have chosen any weapon, but he liked the way a tire iron handled. He could swing it like a bat or use it as a bayonet to stab into a zombie's head to scramble its brain.

Before the Outbreak, necromancers were the only ones who could send a zombie back to its grave. Now, the only way to put them down was to damage the brain so they could no longer function, which was a hell of a lot messier.

He glanced around at the group behind him. Catching Kimber's eyes, he asked, "Are you ready?"

She gave a nod. Reaching out, she clasped Natalie's hand and asked her the same question. Natalie whispered a shaky "Yes" and drew a deep breath. Kimber looked at Duncan. "Let's do this thing," she said and let go of Natalie to grip her hatchet.

She looked determined and brave and scared and too lovely to ignore. He dropped a kiss on her lips.

Her breath hitched then the usual scowl curled her lips. "Don't do that."

He noticed she hadn't moved away from him. Her mouth said

one thing but her actions clearly communicated something else. "Do what?" he asked, letting his hand sweep slowly up her arm.

"Kiss me."

Deliberately misunderstanding, he murmured, "If you insist," and lowered his head to touch his mouth to hers again. Her lips softened under his, coming open on a gasp as he swept his tongue along the seam of her mouth. When he lifted his head she blinked up at him, then the familiar scowl darkened her features. He felt a grin coming and fought it back. Now wasn't the time to continue his assault on the defenses she'd built up against him. They needed to get moving.

"If you two lovebirds are finished, can we maybe go already? I'm really looking forward to fighting off ravenous zombies so we can go cozy up to some hungry vampires."

He slid a glance at Natalie. "Smartass," he muttered. He opened the lock and undid the chain.

Aodhán pushed the gate of the metal fencing open and they all went through, waiting for Duncan to latch the gate before turning toward Main Street. "All right, then," Aodhán said. "I'll be with you for the first mile."

"Are you sure you'll be all right going north on your own?" Kimber asked, her voice soft and concerned. "One of us should go with you."

"I'll move faster on my own, lass." He put a hand on her shoulder. "But I appreciate the offer."

"Let's go," Duncan said. He wasn't worried about Aodhán. The fey could move even faster than vampires; Aodhán could take care of himself. The only reason he was with them was that he owed Duncan, and Duncan had asked him to help protect

Kimber. Right now the sooner they got on their way the sooner they'd know what size horde they faced.

They actually managed to make it two blocks, keeping close to the edges of buildings, skirting around abandoned, rusted vehicles, before they saw the first zombie. And it saw them. They'd been doing this for six months as a team, going out scavenging for supplies, and they had it down pat. Without a word, Duncan kept leading the way while Aodhán headed toward the straggler. He dispatched it in less than a second and rejoined them. He wasn't even breathing hard.

The next ones Duncan heard before he saw them. He held up one hand. Everyone flattened themselves against the nearest building and waited. The shuffling sound of a zombie was distinctive, plus many of them made low grunting or groaning noises when they walked. Not all of them did. Duncan had come to the conclusion that the newly infected were the ones making the noise, as if there was still some part of them inside that recognized what was happening even though they were powerless to stop it.

Or, more prosaically, it could be escaping gas resulting from their decomposition.

He waited until the first dead man lurched around the corner before he acted. He grabbed the zombie's shirt and jerked him around, slamming his back against the wall and the tire iron through his skull in one seamless move. He yanked the weapon out of the zombie and turned to face the next one.

Kimber leaped past him, her hatchet swinging through the air. She buried it in a zombie skull with a low grunt, turning her head to avoid having the spray of blood hit her in the face. She jerked the blade free and watched the corpse hit the ground. She looked at Duncan with a grimace. "Oh, yuck. I really, really hate this." Her voice was quiet but full of revulsion. She tipped her head to one side. "Ew. God, there's something sliding down my neck." The last word was a whispered wail.

He scooped the bit of zombie off her skin and flung it aside. "You're such a girl," he murmured and fought against the urge to kiss her again.

"Shut up. And stop looking at me like that."

"I'd do a lot more than look, if you'd let me," he muttered. Before she could respond, he jerked his head, indicating they should move, and they set off. In another two blocks they killed two more zombies and finally reached the intersection of Main and MLK.

"This is where I say farewell," Aodhán murmured. He and Duncan clasped hands briefly. "I should be home in three or four days."

"Be careful." Kimber moved over to him and threw her arms around his waist, her cheek resting against the muscled chest covered by a thin T-shirt.

The fey warrior's muscled arms returned her hug. "Don't worry about me, *mo chara*. The portal to my people isn't far." He bent his head toward her and smoothed his big hands up and down her back.

Duncan's entire body tightened at the sight of the embrace. It didn't matter that it wasn't sexual in nature. Some other man was touching *his* woman.

His nostrils flared. When had he started thinking of Kimber as his? She wasn't, and while he certainly wanted her, he wasn't planning on anything serious. Or lengthy. He'd learned a long time ago that getting romantically attached to a human never ended well. The human always ended up wanting more than a vampire's nature allowed him to give.

He was the predator; they were the prey. It was the way things had been for centuries. As Kimber and Aodhán's hug continued, Duncan narrowed his eyes. He had no reason to believe anything would be different with Kimber. Or that something would be different for him than it had for any other vampire.

But if that goddamned fairy didn't take his paws off her, he was going to get Duncan's tire iron up his ass.

The two objects of his displeasure drew away from each other, and Duncan relaxed. When he saw the sadness and fear that drew Kimber's pouty mouth into a frown, he tensed again. He understood her concern for Aodhán's safety. Hell, he even shared it. But he didn't have to like it that another man's departure could move her emotions like this.

Shit. He was so twisted up in knots over her, he could feel rage burning deep in his gut. "We need to go," he muttered, taking hold of her elbow, his grip tighter than he meant, but he couldn't make himself let go of her.

Aodhán lifted one brow, then the other when he looked at Duncan's face. The fey warrior's lips pressed together. Duncan shot him a glare, daring Aodhán to comment on the sudden and irrational possessiveness that was holding him so rigid next to Kimber.

"He's right." Aodhán lifted a hand in farewell. "Be careful."

"You, too." Natalie gave him a once over, letting her gaze linger on the large weapon in his hand. "You and your mighty sword."

His lips twitched into a grin. He lifted a hand in silent farewell to Bishop then looked at Kimber. "I'll be back at your place Monday morning, early afternoon at the latest." He glanced at Duncan. "If that's all right with you."

Kimber frowned and tugged on her arm. When Duncan didn't turn her loose, her face deepened into a scowl. "He doesn't have any say, Aodhán. It's your place, too, as long as *you* want it to be."

He dipped his chin in acknowledgment and turned away. Duncan stood with the others and watched him for a few moments then he turned, urging Kimber along with the hand on her arm. "Let's get moving."

The rest of the journey to Maddalene's was strangely anticlimactic. As the gates of her compound were swung open to allow them entrance, Kimber edged closer to Duncan. He caught the dark scent of her fear and put an arm around her. "You'll be safe here, I swear." He glanced over his shoulder at Natalie and Bishop. "All of you."

* * *

Kimber walked alongside Duncan, tucked against his side. She should be more nervous than she was, walking into the lion's den as it were, but with his arm heavy around her shoulders, holding her against him like she was precious cargo, she had a hard time drumming up the appropriate level of anxiety. That wasn't to say she wasn't afraid. She was. Because she wasn't stupid. But Duncan made her feel safe.

Except for that one episode with Maddalene, he always had.

And he always made her want more, especially when he kissed her. She wanted more than she should, more than was possible in this new world. Every day she lived was a day closer to dying. Each time she was victorious over a zombie was one time she was closer to her luck running out.

She'd made all of her friends promise that if she was ever bitten, they'd kill her outright. She'd stared them down until they'd vowed not to wait until she turned. She didn't want them remembering her as a ravening undead creature. They, in turn, had forced the same promise out of her.

But here, with Duncan, she wasn't afraid of zombies, and not just because Maddalene's compound was so secure. She wasn't afraid because she was with him. She just couldn't relax enough to enjoy that feeling or really delve into *why* she felt so safe, especially since in just a few minutes she'd be in the same room with the vampire queen herself.

As they entered the main complex—once an eight-story factory building which had been converted to office space in the nineties, then into condos around 2010—Kimber glanced around at the vampires gathered in the lobby. While she, Natalie, and Bishop weren't as well fed as they had been six months ago before the Outbreak, they were still in much better shape than these guys seemed to be. Some of them looked downright skeletal.

Her brows dipped and she looked up at Duncan's face. He was certainly hale and hearty enough, not appearing to be on the brink of starvation like the others.

At her unspoken question he murmured, "There are perks to being the right-hand of the queen." He dropped his gaze to her. "As long as you're under my protection, you're safe."

She stared into those clear green eyes and wondered how much longer she would benefit from that protection if she didn't do whatever it was that his queen wanted her to do.

How long would it be before they were served up like fatted calves?

Chapter Four

After Natalie and Bishop were ensconced in a very comfortable-looking living room in Duncan's suite, Duncan drew Kimber into another room, this one dominated by a four-poster king-sized bed on a raised platform in front of a large window.

Even while her body quickened with interest, her thoughts winging back to that kiss he'd given her before they'd left her apartment building, her mind balked. "Whoa, now, just wait a minute," she said, pulling her arm away from his light grip.

He flashed her a scowl. "I thought you might like to clean up before you see Maddalene." He gave her that irritating one-shouldered shrug. "But if you'd rather go in with zombie goo on your face and hoodie, that's fine with me."

She was surprised at his thoughtfulness then irritated by her surprise. Duncan, for all his arrogance, had never tried to force her into his bed. It was unjust of her to suspect that would be the first thing he'd do now that he finally had her in his bedroom.

No, when she found herself in his bed, and she had a feeling it wouldn't be much longer because her resistance was waning, it wouldn't be because he had forced her there.

He'd been there for her, through all of this mess, without asking anything of her in return. What more did she think he could do to prove himself? He was her protector, her friend, and only her own stubborn fear over his vampirism kept them apart.

"Sorry," she muttered. Embarrassment made her less than gracious. "It's just…"

Another frown curled his lips down. "Yeah, yeah, I got it, Kimber. You have no interest in sleeping with me." He motioned toward another door. "Bathroom's through there. Clean washcloths and towels are in the linen closet just inside." He turned away. "I'll get you one of my T-shirts to wear."

She reached out and clutched his forearm. "Wait." He paused but didn't turn to face her. She sighed and dropped her hand. "Duncan, I'm sorry. But you keep me so off-kilter, and then drag me into your bedroom…I'm sorry," she said yet again. "I jumped to conclusions."

"Yes, you did." He did turn then, his gaze steady on hers. "Though I will have you in that bed, Kimber. Soon."

His deep voice skimmed over her, electrifying nerve endings that hadn't been alive since before the Outbreak. As his eyes traveled the length of her body, fire raced through her veins. Her heart drummed against her ribs, and as his gaze intensified she could have sworn she felt his big hands stroking her bare skin, urging her to take him deep inside her.

To her relief and disappointment, he shook his head and

added, "Just not today." Regret deepened his tones. "Get that goop washed off. Maddalene's waiting."

Glad to put some distance between them, Kimber went into the bathroom. She closed the door and stripped her hooded sweatshirt over her head. She was happy to see no blood had gotten on her bra. Just the thought of not having that additional barrier, that protection, was more than she wanted to think about now. She couldn't handle Duncan knowing she was naked beneath one of his shirts. That the only obstruction between her nipples and his hands, his mouth, would be one thin cotton tee.

Beneath the sheer white satin of her bra, her nipples tightened into hard buds. Traitors. They knew what they wanted, regardless of how hard Kimber fought against it. "But you can't have it," she muttered at her chest.

She sighed. It was official. The zombie apocalypse had turned her into a loon. She was standing there talking to her boobs. But just because she hadn't had sex in more years than she cared to count, hadn't had a decent orgasm in over a year except by her own hand—never mind that she'd fantasized it was Duncan doing carnal, dark things to her—didn't mean she had to keep lusting after him. Even if he was such a sexy, sexy man.

"Just forget about it," she told her nipples and her now-thudding clit. With another sigh she grabbed a washcloth from the narrow linen closet next to the toilet and wet it. She had just rinsed it out the final time and was craning her neck to make sure she'd gotten all the blood off when knuckles rapped on the door. Before she could say anything, the door opened far enough for Duncan to reach his arm through, a navy blue T-shirt dangling from his fist.

"Thanks," she said as she took it from his grip.

"No problem."

The door closed and she stood a moment, staring down at the soft cotton in her hand before slowly bringing it to her face and breathing in through her nose. The shirt smelled fresh, no lingering scent of Duncan on it anywhere. Of course he would give her a clean shirt, but she couldn't deny the disappointment that rolled through her. With a muttered curse she dragged it over her head. The shoulder seams came halfway down her upper arms, and the sleeves ended below her elbows.

She opened the door and saw Duncan standing next to the bed, staring down at its surface. When she walked into the room he turned, and she bit back a gasp at the raw sensual hunger in his eyes. The look vanished in a second, replaced by the indolent arrogance she was used to seeing.

"Ready?" he asked. His deep baritone husked across her nerve endings, setting up a shiver along her spine and a dull throb in her nether region.

She drew a bracing breath. "As ready as I'll ever be," she responded, happy to hear her voice was mostly steady. "Let's get it over with."

They walked back into the living room. Natalie and Bishop looked up. Kimber noticed a wood fire blazing in the fireplace. Duncan must have started it after she'd gone into the bedroom. It was cool in the room and would get even colder as the night wore on. It had been a thoughtful gesture for him to provide warmth for her friends.

"You'll be safe here," Duncan told them. "I'll have two guards posted outside."

"We're prisoners then?" Natalie asked, her tone challenging.

"Do you really think it would be a good idea for either of you to wander off?" he asked, his voice cool, unfazed by her defiance.

She scowled. "No." She crossed her arms over her breasts and glared at him.

His shoulders lifted with his sigh. "Look," he said, running one big hand through his dark hair, "I know you're nervous about being here. But I give you my word, you're safe. The men outside that door will fight to the death to protect you." He looked at Kimber. "Let's go."

She exchanged glances with her friends then took the hand Duncan offered and let him draw her out of the room. She tried to ignore the way his cool flesh warmed from the contact with her skin, tried to ignore how good his slightly callused palm felt clasped within her hand. Tried to ignore the fluttering of need low in her belly. She had other things to focus on, things that could get her killed if she wasn't paying close enough attention.

They walked down the hallway to the next door across the hall. Duncan rapped twice with two knuckles. "This is convenient," Kimber sniped. "You being just across the hall from her." It wasn't jealousy flaring, she told herself. Why should it matter to her how close Duncan's suite was to his queen's? He was her second in command, after all. It would make sense they would live close together.

His only response to her comment was to slant a dry glance her way. As the door opened and they entered, she took a few seconds to look around. At one time she supposed it had been a separate condo, but now it served as Maddalene's throne room. That was the only way Kimber could describe it. Gleaming hardwood covered the floor and a floor-to-ceiling window along the southern wall made the space look larger than it was. Heavy dark green drapes hung on each side of the window, ready to be drawn to protect Maddalene against the sun once daybreak came.

There was a small seating area near a raised platform that held, instead of a throne, a plush aubergine chaise, upon which the queen of the vampires lounged like a, well, queen. Two tall, muscled men clad only in black boxer briefs stood slightly behind the chaise, one on each side like hunky bookends.

"Kimberly!" Maddalene rose to her feet in a fluid move and glided forward, hands outstretched. She wore a long black dress that was sleeveless with a high collar. Her dark hair was piled on top of her head in an intricate up-do. All in all, she defined elegance. "I'm so happy you were able to visit."

Inherent good manners and a healthy streak of common sense made Kimber clasp Maddalene's hands and let the vampire brush air kisses near one and then the other cheek. "I wasn't aware I had a choice," Kimber murmured as the vampire queen let go of her hands and took a step back.

The ready smile that curved lusciously painted red lips didn't reflect in her nearly black eyes. "My impatience got the best of me, I'm afraid. I've been trying to see you for so long."

"And now you have." Kimber ignored Duncan's warning glance. She was through with the social amenities. "So what can I do for you?"

"To the point. I like that." Maddalene walked back to the chaise and settled onto it with such a graceful move that Kimber felt like a lumbering elephant in comparison. The vampire queen studied her a moment and beckoned to the man on her left.

"These are my pets," she said as he went to his knees in front of her. "Well fed and cared for."

Even from where she stood Kimber could see the many puckered scars on his neck and forearms. Maddalene stroked from his shoulder down to his hand and then brought his wrist to her mouth. She bit down. He gave a low grunt and then a soft groan. Maddalene fed from him a moment, her gaze never leaving Kimber. The vampire released the man and waved him away. He retook his stance behind her, looking a little pale, but he seemed steady enough on his feet. His cock was a hard ridge beneath the cotton of his boxers.

Kimber had known there was a sexual element to a vampire's bite. She just hadn't seen it demonstrated before now. She clenched her jaw and fought against sidling closer to Duncan. It would be a show of weakness. She wasn't sure why Maddalene had decided to feed in front of her, other than to freak her out.

The vampire queen stared at her a few more seconds and seemed to come to some kind of decision. She gave a short nod and said, "I'll be just as direct as you. I want you to raise someone from the dead."

Kimber crossed her arms and stared at the other woman. "Why me? If all you needed was a necromancer, there are others that can take care of a Lazarus."

A slight smile edged Maddalene's full lips. "Ah, but this isn't just any Lazarus. This one died a human death over a hundred years ago." Her gaze became tinged with silver. "And for his raising I want the best. Which is you."

Kimber felt Duncan stiffen next to her, but she didn't look away from the vampire queen. "It can't be done," Kimber said, shaking her head. "And even if it could be, it's a really bad idea. A really, really, really bad idea."

"Why?"

"When we raise someone from the dead, someone who's newly dead," she stressed, "there's still a spark of their soul left behind, something that the Unseen can latch onto in order to reanimate the corpse." She turned her attention back to Maddalene. "But with someone who's been dead for over a hundred years..." She shook her head. "It would take too much of the Unseen for reanimation to occur," she protested, not adding that it might very well drive her insane. She had the feeling Maddalene wouldn't care about that. "What was brought back wouldn't necessarily be that person. There might be a spark of a soul left to attach to, but not enough."

"I couldn't care less about his soul," the vampire queen said. "I just want him."

"Who?" Kimber asked.

"That is irrelevant to you." Maddalene's tone was as imperious as Kimber had ever heard it. "What is relevant is what I can do for you if you perform this one task for me."

Kimber had no interest in trying to raise a century-old corpse, but she was curious as to what bribe Maddalene thought to offer. "And what would that be?" Kimber asked.

"Protection for you and your friends. Safe passage anywhere in the city, with my vampires keeping the zombies at bay. Or, if you'd prefer, a guarantee of your safety to stay here. With Duncan." Her gaze cut to her second in command and one perfectly shaped eyebrow rose.

It shouldn't have surprised her that Maddalene knew about

Duncan's desire for her. But it did. And it unsettled her.

"That's a tempting offer," Kimber said truthfully. To get even one night's sleep without waking because of the worry zombies would break in was more attractive than she wanted to admit out loud. "But I'm sorry. It can't be done. It *shouldn't* be done."

Maddalene's eyes narrowed and irritation shot silver through her dark irises. She beckoned to the man on her right and, when he knelt before her, she leaned over to whisper in his ear. He inclined his head. He stood and walked out of the room, closing the door softly behind him.

"Then let me amend my offer," Maddalene said in a soft voice that nevertheless held steely determination. "Do this for me, or you and your friends' lives will be forfeit."

Ice slide down Kimber's spine and spread through her belly.

"No! Maddalene, you've gone too far." Duncan took a step forward. "We've talked about this—"

"And the time for talk has passed." The vampire queen rose to her feet and stared down at Kimber. "I will give you forty-eight hours to think on this, Kimberly. After that, your fate and that of your friends is in my hands. Whatever the outcome, know that it's because of your decision." She waved one hand. "You may rejoin your friends while Duncan and I chat further."

Kimber fought down her panic and left the room without looking at Duncan. She was afraid of what she'd see—either a reassuring glance that wouldn't convince her, or an expression of frustration and dismay that would only increase her own alarm. As soon as she left Maddalene's chambers she realized that the two vampires who'd been guarding the door to Duncan's suite were no longer there. "Shit," she muttered and sprinted to Duncan's. With another grumbled imprecation, she threw open the door. Natalie and Bishop both looked up from where they were still seated, alive and well, on the sofa. Relief weakened her knees so that she almost fell. She closed the door behind her.

"What is it?" Natalie cried out, jumping to her feet. She rushed over to Kimber and grabbed her arm. "What's wrong?"

"The guards are gone," Kimber whispered. "I was afraid…"

"We're fine," Bishop said, coming over to them. "We didn't even know they were gone." He glanced at Natalie and then looked at Kimber again. "I wonder why they left."

Kimber remembered the vampire queen sending the human out of the room. "I think Maddalene's making a point," she said softly. She wandered over to the sofa and plopped down. The other two sat beside her. "She wants me to resurrect a Lazarus that's over a hundred years old."

"What?" Natalie leaned back against the arm of the couch. "She can't be serious. No one's ever raised one that old."

"And there's a good reason why," Kimber said. "I've only once had to reanimate someone who'd been dead twenty years, and I slept for a week afterward. Well, when the nightmares would let me sleep."

"Nightmares?" Bishop asked, bracing an arm against one thigh.

While Bishop had seen her in action as a necromancer, he'd never seen the aftermath. "Whenever I tap into the Unseen," she told him, "I have nightmares afterward. Most necromancers do. I think it's the residual magic of that plane lingering inside me, and it has to have an outlet." She gave a slight shrug. "Apparently terror works well."

"I had no idea." Bishop leaned toward her. "And if you tried to reanimate a corpse that's over a hundred years old?"

Kimber shook her head. "I don't even want to think about it," she said with a sigh. "That week, the one where I had nightmares every time I fell asleep…I thought I was going to lose my mind."

She didn't want to think about that week. It had been before the Outbreak, before Duncan had come into her life. It had been just her and Natalie, and thank God Natalie had been there with her, soothing her every time she screamed herself awake. She never wanted to go through that again. Ever.

She glanced at her friends. "To do what Maddalene wants me to, I'd have to tap so deep into the Unseen, I don't know if I'd survive it." She glanced at her friends. "At least not with my sanity intact."

Before either of her friends could respond, the door opened. Rather than Duncan, three gaunt, red-eyed-with-hunger vamps walked into the room.

"Oh, shit," Natalie breathed.

Kimber agreed completely.

* * *

"You've gone too far, Maddalene." Duncan paced in front of her chaise. "Threatening Kimber and her friends isn't the way to get her to cooperate."

"I think it's the perfect way." The vampire queen's upper lip lifted in a snarl, showing the sharp tips of her fangs. "If I cannot cajole her cooperation, I'll coerce it." She stabbed her forefinger at him. "And you will help."

"No."

Her eyes narrowed. "I think I misheard you, my sweet. What did you say?"

"You heard me right, Maddalene. I'm not going to coerce Kimber into raising Eduardo for you. I'm not even sure it can be done, especially now. It's the magic of the Unseen that has given us our current zombie…problem. We ourselves are nothing but reanimated corpses, perhaps even by the same magic."

"Exactly! Zombies have no real impact on our way of life. There are still plenty of humans to go around. Why, we could even offer them a safe haven from the hordes. For a price of blood of course. This may have been the best thing that could have happened to us!"

She was crazy. He'd suspected it before, more than once, but for her to think that the zombie apocalypse was good for vampires was the ultimate insanity.

"We are of the Unseen; you said it yourself. Don't you see, Duncan, why it would be possible, then?" She stood and glided off the platform to stand in front of him, blocking him from pacing, and stroked her hand down his forearm to clasp his hand. Her slender hand felt frail curled around his, but he knew she had preternatural strength equal to or perhaps even greater than his. She'd never told him her age, but he knew she was old. Much older than he was. He had never underestimated her and he wasn't about to now.

"What are you talking about?" he asked.

"If we are animated by the Unseen, then Eduardo can be brought back. Returned to me as if our enemies had never taken him away. And he can celebrate their demise with me."

"But why, Maddalene?" He kept his voice gentle and let some of his confusion show through. "He's been gone a year now. I thought you'd come to terms with his true death."

Her eyes snapped with heat. "Never. I will never accept his true death. He is my mate, Duncan. My partner." She dropped his hand and returned to her chaise. As she settled on it, she waved one hand in dismissal. "And you will assist in his return."

He ground his jaw. There was no talking to her when she went into her regal mode. He'd have to find another way. With a bow of his head, he turned and left the room. As he entered the empty hallway, he frowned. Where were the two guards he'd assigned to his quarters? He ran the few yards to his door and flung it open. He roared at what he saw.

Three emaciated vampires surrounded Kimber, Natalie, and Bishop. Kimber held one of the fire pokers, Bishop had taken up a burning log, and Natalie had her short sword. They appeared unharmed and relief mingled with his rage.

At Duncan's entry the vampires turned and shrunk back from him. "These humans are here under my protection," he said as he stalked forward. He curled his fingers into his palms. "Get out."

They hesitated. One of them eyed Kimber and ran his tongue over his cracked lips. "But the queen told us—"

Duncan snarled, showing his fangs, and grabbed the vamp. With a quick wrench he broke the vampire's neck and let the body fall. The broken neck would heal, but with the vampire as underfed as he was it would take a long time. Duncan looked at the other two. "Would either of you care to tell me what the queen said?" When they shook their heads, he motioned to the body on the floor. "Take your friend and get out. And from now on my quarters are off limits to you."

"Yes, sir." They grabbed their fallen comrade beneath his arms and dragged him out of the room.

Duncan looked at Kimber and the others. "Let's get out of here."

Bishop tossed the log back into the fireplace, though Kimber held on to the poker. Her hatchet still hung from one of her belt loops. The three humans followed Duncan out of the room and exited the complex without question. Once they were near the front gates, Kimber asked, "What the hell was that all about? I thought you said we'd be safe there."

His jaw tightened but he didn't respond.

Kimber grabbed his arm. "Duncan. You *said* we'd be safe."

When he looked at her, he knew his eyes had gone silver with rage, knew that his irises were rimmed with crimson. Not all of it was fury. Some of it was good old-fashioned lust, the desire to take his woman and claim her, to pierce her with fangs and cock. "I will die before I let something happen to you." His voice was guttural, nearly inhuman.

Damn Maddalene. Damn her and her ill-advised quest. Damn his own need. He would protect Kimber from the other vampires, but who would protect her from him?

Chapter Five

So what did Maddalene say?" Kimber asked Duncan, keeping her voice low as they made their way back to the apartment complex. It was still dark, though the moon was bright enough that they didn't need to use their flashlights. She glanced over her shoulder to make sure Natalie and Bishop were still right behind them.

Duncan shook his head and refused to answer her question.

She frowned up at him. "What, it's top secret?"

"Something like that," he muttered.

"Frickin' vampires," she responded in a grumble. She glanced at him. "Did she really mean for those vamps to chow down on us, or was she just showing me that they could?"

"It was a demonstration of power." His green eyes glittered with shards of vampire silver. "She wouldn't dare harm someone I've placed under my protection."

She stared at him. "Are you sure about that? Because that wasn't the impression I got." She started to say more but stopped when he held up a hand. Then she heard them. Zombies. A lot of them.

The sound they made was like the air escaping from rotted bagpipes. Dull and monotonous, a broken sound, an unnatural sound, and it was getting louder. Closer.

Shit.

They were still at least a mile away from her apartment building, and at least that far from the vampire conclave. Caught in the middle, two directions they could go, and from the sound of things they were going to have to fight their way through zombies regardless of which way they headed. She caught Duncan's glance. "My place," she whispered even as she knew she had to let the others give their input. But she sure as hell wasn't ready to head back into vamp city to be subjected to another demonstration of just how easily she and her friends could become vampire Slurpees.

She sidled up next to Duncan, pressed against the side of the old headquarters of a bank. A tattered and faded poster from the CDC stuck to the brick. Some bastard had had a sense of humor, plastering a *Don't be a zombie, be prepared* poster on the wall. The CDC had put those together for fun, and at the time Kimber had appreciated the sense of humor. She didn't so much now.

She peered around the corner of a building. At least twenty, maybe as many as thirty zombies shuffled forward, mouths wide open, arms outstretched. Rotting remnants of clothing hung from emaciated, decaying flesh. Their putrid stench was overpowering, filling her nose. Bile rose in her throat.

Swallowing, she battled back the urge to vomit and glanced over her shoulder. God. At least as many of the undead shufflers were coming up from behind them. She glanced at Natalie and jerked her head to direct her friend's attention behind them.

"Oh, my God," the other woman whispered. "Where's that damn fairy and his mighty sword when you need him?" Her gaze darted over the horde. Face paling, she gasped. *"Oh-godohgodwe'regonnadie."*

Bishop's jaw flexed. "Leave the hysterics up to me, would you? I've got it down to a science." His voice never wavered from the calm, collected tones he was known for.

Duncan raised an eyebrow but otherwise didn't comment.

Kimber did her best to ignore the antics of both of them. "We either head forward to the safety of the apartment," she whispered, "or go back to Maddalene's."

"I vote to go forward," Bishop muttered. His hard gaze suggested he was as unwilling to provide a meal for the hungry vamps as she was.

"Me, too," Natalie said softly.

Duncan blew out a sigh. "Let's go, then." His silvered eyes flicked to each of them. "Stay close. Do not get separated from the group."

Facing a horde alone was almost certainly a death sentence. The old adage "safety in numbers" had never been truer than it was in the zombie apocalypse.

They moved forward as a cohesive unit. With Duncan in the lead, they cut a swath through the horde in front. At one point Kimber became trapped against the rusted frame of an old Buick, holding a female zombie away with stiffened arms against the emaciated shoulders, unable to bring the fire poker up to defend herself.

Duncan yanked the zombie away from Kimber and drove his crowbar through the undead thing's forehead. He let the body drop to the ground and grabbed Kimber's hand. "Stop fucking around," he muttered.

She shot him a glare. "Give me a break. It's not like I was playing with her."

One corner of his sensual mouth kicked up in a grin. God. Even with zombies all around, his good looks made her breath hitch in her throat. *Not now, Kimber.*

Grumbling, she rushed the next zombie and the next, until they were down to only about half a dozen between them and the safety of the apartment complex. She glanced behind her to see those zombies were still shuffling forward. "Let's make tracks, people," she yelled.

Bishop dispatched a zombie and, as the body fell, he shouted, "Hoo-frickin'-yah!"

Duncan and Natalie took out a zombie each. Kimber shoved the fire poker through the eye of another one, cursing when the hooked end got hung up in the skull. Muttering another flaming cuss word, she let go of the poker and slid her hatchet from her belt.

She took out another shuffler and was just starting to look around to check on Bishop when she heard him cry out. She whirled to see him holding a zombie away from him with one arm, but another of the creatures had latched onto the opposite shoulder with its teeth. Blood stained his shirt, the material ripped. Even from where she was she could see the zombie's teeth embedded deep into the muscles of Bishop's shoulder.

Oh, God.

As Kimber rushed forward, the zombie jerked its head, ripping away a mouthful of Bishop's flesh. Kimber screamed. She plunged her hatchet into its forehead and pulled the dead thing off him just as Duncan took out the second one. From her peripheral vision she saw Natalie stab her short sword upward through the mouth of the final zombie standing between them and safety.

Duncan threw Bishop over his shoulder. "Come on!" He took off in a loping run, not using his vampire speed so that Kimber and Natalie could keep up with him.

No one said a word until they had latched the outer gate of the apartment complex behind them and Duncan gently set Bishop on the ground, leaning him back against the side of the apartment building. Bishop's face was gray, his mouth taut with pain. Eyes closed, his breath came in labored pants.

Kimber dropped to her knees beside him. "Carson…"

His eyes fluttered open. "It must be bad." His grin was more of a grimace and it broke her heart. "You've never used my first name before."

She blinked back tears. She wasn't going to lose him, damn it. Too many people, good people, had died, and it was all her fault. Her throat closed up, the guilt bubbling up in the form of bitter bile.

No! Carson Bishop wasn't going to be another name added to the list of people who were dead because of her. Hell, no.

"Kimber, you know what needs to be done." Duncan's deep voice rasped from behind her, and she realized he'd knelt behind her.

"No." Her voice cracked, the sound as brittle as broken glass.

"Honey…" Natalie went to her knees on Bishop's other side. She took Bishop's hand in hers before her gaze went back to Kimber. "He's gonna turn."

Kimber shook her head. A tear plopped onto her cheek and began a slow glide down her face.

"She's right." Bishop's voice wavered. His Adam's apple bobbed with his hard swallow. Sweat beaded on his forehead, above his mouth. "I already have a fever and my joints are starting to ache. It's just a matter of time before I'm dead, and then…" His mouth thinned. Eyes dark with dread, he said, "I'll turn into one of them." He jerked his head to where a few zombies pressed against the metal fencing that surrounded the complex. "I don't want you—any of you—to see me like that. Kill me now."

"No!" Kimber swiped her face. "I can fix this. Fix you."

Duncan put one hand on her shoulder. "Sweetheart, there isn't a cure."

Kimber shrugged off his hand. She wasn't going to lose her friend. She just wasn't. She put a hand on Bishop's shoulder, just to one side of the injury, and closed her eyes. With a deep breath, she reached for the Unseen. She'd never done it before without first setting a circle of blood, but she was desperate. Bishop's own bloody wound might be enough. It would *have* to be enough. She refused to let him die.

"Kimber…" Duncan's voice trailed off.

The fine hairs on the back of her neck lifted as the power of the Unseen surged into her. Good. That was good. She kept her hand on Bishop's shoulder and concentrated on his wound. "I started this, Duncan, six months ago when I tapped into the Unseen and animated Richard Whitcomb. What if I can reverse it?" She blinked her burning eyes, refusing to let any more tears fall. "I have to try."

"You *have* tried before, without success. Right after the Outbreak happened, then a month later, and a month after that." He paused then added softly, "Sweetheart, there's nothing you can do for him."

The compassion in his voice ate at her composure and a sob broke out before she ruthlessly forced her emotions back. "I have to try," she said again, her voice rasping with the truth she refused to acknowledge. She ground her teeth, the muscles in her jaw aching with the strain.

"Kimber, Duncan's right," Bishop whispered. "I can't feel my legs. You know how this progresses. I only have a few minutes."

"No!" She fixed her attention on the Unseen again, and it surged into her in a rush that stole her breath. She pushed it toward the wound on Bishop's shoulder, could almost see the energy flow over his skin, into the bite marks. It swirled into his muscles, making him cry out in agony. As the energy continued to crash over her in undulating waves, she couldn't contain her own moan of pain. As nerve endings enflamed and muscles screamed with tension, she closed her eyes to shut off at least one of her senses.

Then, bit by bit, she began to draw the energy away from Bishop and direct it back into the Unseen. Hit by this much power, the muscles along her back, her thighs and calves, seized up in one big, vicious cramp. She gasped but kept drawing the energy from Bishop, doing her best to ignore the increasing torment. From behind her closed lids red hazed her vision, then black, and dots of light began floating through the darkness.

Vaguely she heard Duncan and Natalie calling her name. Her hand clutched Bishop's shoulder in a spasm. Even through the physical pain, she could feel that what she was doing was working. The Unseen was withdrawing, taking the supernatural venom of the zombie's bite from Bishop. Just a little more. Just a little…

Her heart stuttered. The floating dots multiplied and then winked out like candles snuffed by a fierce wind. Her pulse thundered in her ears then slowed, sounding like thick sludge sliding down a drain.

Suddenly she was knocked away from Bishop. "No!" she screamed, opening her eyes to see Duncan's face, his eyes blazing with silver fire. "I'm not done." She reached for Bishop again.

Duncan whirled her away from the wounded man and wrapped his arms around her from behind, his big hands holding her wrists, keeping her arms bent in front of her. For all his gentleness, she couldn't break free.

"Let me go." She struggled anyway. "I need to help Bishop."

"He's beyond your help, sweetheart." Duncan rested his cheek against the top of her head. With his next words his breath stirred her hair. "He's beyond anyone's help now. He's gone."

She couldn't stop the tears now. "No…" She slumped in his embrace. Her body burned—eyes stinging with tears, muscles blazing with tension, mind flaming with yet another failure. A personal one this time. With a surge of strength she twisted in his arms and slapped him. "Why did you stop me? It was working. I could have saved him." Her voice broke on a sob. She lifted her hand and slapped him again, harder this time. His head turned with the force of the hit, but when he looked down at her she saw no anger, no condemnation for her action. Just tender sadness and understanding.

"It was killing you," came Natalie's soft, sorrowful voice.

Kimber looked at her friend, who nodded.

"Your heart stopped beating twice," Duncan murmured. The reddened imprint of her fingers against his cheek showed starkly against his skin before it faded. "It started up on its own, but then your blood pressure shot up and then dropped so low…" He cleared his throat. "If I hadn't pulled you away, you would have died. And that I'm not prepared to let happen."

"But…" She stared down at Bishop. His sightless eyes gazed at nothing, and as she watched tiny flecks of color began swirling in his irises. Already the small bit of the Unseen left in him was gathering strength, readying his body to be transformed into one of the walking dead.

She'd failed. Again. And this time it had mattered, more than at any other time. She'd started it and once again she'd been unable to stop it.

Everything inside her shut down. Her hearing became muffled, her vision clouded, her body went numb. The brief realization that she was in shock rolled through her thoughts before those, too, went blessedly silent.

"Natalie," she heard Duncan murmur. She saw the crowbar gripped in his hand and knew what he was going to do.

Kimber felt Natalie put an arm around her waist, drawing her away. She made a sound of protest, something like a grunt or maybe it was closer to a whimper, but couldn't find the strength to fight the sympathetic hold. Her head felt light, like it would float away, and her legs and arms shook with little tremors. With a final glance at Bishop's face, those lifeless, staring eyes, she let Natalie lead her away.

* * *

Duncan closed the door of Kimber's apartment behind him and flipped the lock. Without looking at the two women, he headed toward the bathroom. Once he'd cleaned himself up and wiped the blood off the crowbar, he went back into the living room where Kimber and Natalie sat on the sofa. They'd both kicked off their shoes. "It's done," he said, knowing they had both realized what he'd been about to do, knowing he didn't need to tell them, but still he'd felt the need to say it out loud.

Natalie gave a brief nod and stood. "I'm going to clean up and go to bed." She glanced at Kimber. "I won't use all the hot water, I promise."

Kimber didn't respond to the mellow joke. Natalie met his eyes, hers filled with concern.

"I'll take care of her," he promised.

She gave a nod and left the living room.

Duncan sat beside Kimber and put an arm around her shoulders. He pulled her to his side, wishing his body held heat like a human's so he could warm her, console her. The fact that she didn't fight the little bit of comfort he tried to give told him clearly how defeated she felt at the moment. She remained stiff, not relaxing into his light hold at all. She seemed to be regaining some vitality, because color had seeped back into skin that had gone gray with the energy she'd used to tap into the Unseen.

They sat like that for several minutes. The sound of the shower shut off—a record short time for Natalie—and then the bath-room door opened. He heard her patter to the bedroom she and Kimber shared, and that door closed.

Duncan rubbed his palm up and down Kimber's upper arm, lending his silent support as she processed Bishop's death. Finally she took a shuddering breath and settled against him. She turned slightly, winding one arm behind his back and the other across his waist, turning his one-armed hug into a true embrace.

"I'm sorry for hitting you," she whispered. She rubbed her face against his shoulder. "I know it wasn't your fault."

Duncan brought his left arm over her and clasped his hands together. He rested his cheek against the top of her head. "It wasn't your fault, either."

She stiffened slightly. "If I hadn't—"

"No, Kimber." He tightened his hold. "Enough. You can't keep blaming yourself for creating this mess. Even if you somehow caused it through your necromancy, you didn't do it on purpose." He paused. "Unless you have some secret take-over-the-world plan I don't know anything about."

She snorted a laugh. "No. No plans to take over the world with my zombie hordes."

"Good to know." He could feel the slight tremble going through her body and knew the lingering effects of shock contin-ued to affect her. "Come on," he said, standing and drawing her to her feet.

"Where're we going?" She swayed, clutching at his arms for balance.

"You're going to take a shower." He swept her up into his arms and strode down the hallway. He didn't set her down until he reached the bathroom. He reached into the shower and turned on the water, adjusting it until it was warm enough, then turned back to her. She stood where he'd placed her, blinking up at him. He stroked the back of his hand down her satiny cheek. "Go on, then," he murmured. "Get your clothes off and hop in." He turned to leave.

"Duncan." Her scratchy voice stopped him.

He looked at her. Her eyes beseeched him, tugged at a heart he'd long ago been certain he'd squandered. "What is it, sweetheart?"

"I don't want to be alone."

The brokenness in her voice broke the heart he'd just rediscovered. "Kimber, if I get naked with you..." He wanted her. But he wasn't going to take advantage of her trauma. She'd lost a good friend and wasn't thinking things through. If she were, the last person on the planet with whom she'd want to be nude was him. She'd always been very clear about that. He shook his head. "Just take a shower. I'll be in the living room when you're done."

He started to leave the bathroom again but she called him back. "I *want* you to get naked with me," she whispered.

Shock made him draw a reflexive and unnecessary breath. It didn't, however, keep him from getting an erection. He slowly moved to face her again. He wasn't so noble that he could continue to turn her down. He wanted her to be very sure about what she was asking of him, what consequences would come of her request. "If we're both naked, I'm going to fuck you," he said, his voice and words raw and needy. His fangs elongated, the slight prick of them against his lip a reminder of how far gone he was already. "It won't be slow and gentle. I've waited too long. I'm so desperate to get inside you that I'll fuck you hard and fast. I'll work my cock so deep you'll feel me against your womb."

Her pupils dilated. She bit her bottom lip but met his gaze head-on. "I don't want slow. I don't want gentle. I need hard and fast and desperate." She pulled his T-shirt over her head and dropped it to the floor. The upper swells of her breasts gleamed pale against the soft lace of her bra.

He watched with burning eyes as she flipped the button at the waist of her low-slung jeans and slid down the zipper. She wiggled them down her hips and stepped out of them. When her hands went behind her back and unhooked her bra, thrusting her breasts out, blood pulsed in his cock. And when she shrugged out of the bra and he saw her bare breasts with their pink-tipped nipples, a groan rumbled from his chest. He'd wanted so long to see her like this, his self-control, his sense of right and wrong was being quickly overridden by the need pulsing in his cock and fangs.

He stepped forward and palmed one plump mound. Her nipple peaked against his hand. "Be sure," he said, his gaze holding hers.

"Take a shower with me." She pressed his hand harder against her. "Take me."

Chapter Six

There was a part of Kimber that wanted to remain frozen behind the grief and shock of Bishop's death, but her overriding desire for Duncan meant she couldn't hold back any longer. In a very visceral way, Bishop's death had forced her to realize how short life was, how quickly everything that mattered to her could be taken.

She wouldn't hide behind the lies anymore. She did want him. She'd wanted him from the moment she'd first seen him, with those glass green eyes, handsome face, broad shoulders and long, lean body. Even his bossy, arrogant attitude had wormed its way into her heart. With death waiting for her outside, she decided for once she was going to follow her desire instead of listening to her mind.

She slipped her hands beneath his shirt, spreading her fingers along his back and pressing the tips into soft skin covering hard muscles. With a grunt of impatience he stripped the shirt off, letting it drop on the floor. With one booted heel he closed the bathroom door.

Reaching out, he traced a fingertip down her cheek. "So soft," he whispered. With efficiency he'd soon stripped himself. His shoulders were wide, his chest broad and sculpted, tapering to a slim waist. The muscles of his stomach redefined washboard. Just being with him made her feel safe, and that was something she'd never truly felt anywhere else.

He was beautiful. And right now, in this moment, he was hers. There were no promises for tomorrow. Nothing else mattered, just this. Her heart beat heavily. Every sense heightened, and she was helpless to prevent her heart's fast slide for this man. It would be so easy to fall in love with him. Hell, maybe she already had taken the plunge. She'd think about that later. Much, much later.

Big hands swept her panties down and off her legs, and he moved her under the warm spray of the shower. Despite the hard prod of his cock at her back, he seemed in no hurry to follow through on his promise. Instead, he pressed a kiss to her shoulder. "Let me bathe you."

Kimber gave a small nod. She was tired. Tired of battling zombies, tired of always being strong, tired of fighting her feelings for Duncan. For once she would let him take care of her.

He took his time washing her body. His broad palms spread vanilla-scented lather over her skin, reaching from behind to follow the curves of her breasts and the slight slope of her belly. They skated down her legs to her feet. She braced her hands against the wall of the shower and lifted one foot and then the other while he washed between her toes. Then he soaped his hands again and washed her arms, then her back. He urged her back under the spray and rinsed the soap off.

"I think you missed a couple of spots," she murmured. While

his gentle touch soothed her—and surprised her, to be honest—it also heightened her desire. Her voice came out sultry, throaty. He hadn't touched where she needed it most, the throbbing, wet flesh between her thighs.

"Patience." He worked strawberry-scented shampoo into a thick lather in her hair, his fingers massaging her head and neck until she nearly went boneless against him. "I love your hair. Did I ever tell you that?"

"No."

"I do." His strong hands worked the lather through her tresses. "It's such a fiery color. And the length is perfect."

"Perfect for what?" She leaned into him, her back against his chest, her hands resting on his thick thighs.

He wrapped it around his hand and lightly tugged her head back until it rested on his shoulder. Her pulse thudded at the aggressive show of dominance. It should have scared her, but it didn't. It sent licks of sensual excitement through her body, centering between her thighs.

When he moved her back into the spray to rinse her hair, she turned in his loose hold and looped her arms around his neck. Her extreme tiredness had vanished, purged by her surging arousal. She couldn't resist the urge to tease him. "What happened to hard and fast and desperate?" she asked, arching one brow at him.

His smile was slow and so full of male arrogance and desire it made her chest hurt. "I managed to find a bit of restraint. I know," he said with false modesty, "I surprise even myself."

His hands cupped her breasts and massaged gently, tweaking her nipples and lifting them up as an offering to his waiting lips.

His tongue sent lightning from her nipple to her clit, and she began to pant. She grabbed his biceps and held on as his tongue caused wave after wave to crash through her body. He let go of one to move to the other and begin all over again. She begged and pleaded, though she wasn't sure exactly what she was pleading for. For him to stop? For him to do more? Both?

Finally, after several moments of play at her breasts he moved farther down to her stomach. He rinsed the soap off one hand and moved it between her thighs, sliding his fingers through the folds of her sex. A long finger stroked across her swollen clit. She gasped and moved her hands to his shoulders. He slid his other hand into the crack of her ass, the pad of his thumb rubbing over her sensitive rosebud. "There's a lot to be said for anticipation," he murmured.

From somewhere she managed to get a hold of a measure of fair play and decided it was time to take him in hand. "Yes, I agree." She squirted a good amount of shower gel in the palm of her hand. "Let me return the favor."

She washed him just as thoroughly as he had her, and when she got to his hard cock, she perched on the built-in corner bench and beckoned him closer. His broad shoulders blocked the spray of water though rivulets ran in tiny streams down his chest. Now that the warm water no longer sluiced directly on her, the chill of the room made her nipples pucker. She shivered, wanting his mouth on her, but decided she wanted to test that vaunted restraint he'd claimed to have found.

Kimber pressed her mouth to his corded abdomen, tracing the lines of Duncan's six pack with her tongue. As she breathed against his belly, his muscles quivered, his cock bobbing up to butt against her chin. "I guess you like that." She smiled against him and traced the tip of her tongue around the indent of his navel. "How do you like this?" she asked.

"Lower," he instructed, his voice harsh and tight. His hands came up to fist in her hair.

She cleared her throat. Pitching her voice deep, she asked again, "How do you like this?"

"Smartass," he muttered. And laughed. It was gruff, rusty, like it was something he didn't do often. And he probably didn't. In all the time she'd known him, the only time she'd seen him smile was when he was giving her a hard time.

She cupped his sac and stroked his hard shaft. He pulsed in her hand, his skin ruddy and hot from the water. His arousal forced blood to flow and warm his body. She wet her lips and wrapped them around the head of his cock.

He moaned and sifted his fingers through her hair. "Oh, Kimber. Shit!"

She did a little moaning herself and took him deeper. His flesh was hot and hard, her saliva making his shaft shiny with each outstroke. She fondled his balls in her hand, rolling them over her fingers, tugging on them with firm but gentle pressure.

He let loose with a string of expletives. She would have smiled if she could have around the stalk of flesh in her mouth. So much for his vaunted self-control.

As she took him as deep as she could, he cried out in surprise. His hips bucked. The head of his cock nudged the back of her throat. She relaxed her jaw and held him there a moment before humming loudly. His groan was more of a feral growl, full of pleasure and lust. Fingers tightening in her hair, he pulled back from her mouth a little. He took control then, his hips pumping as he worked his cock in and out of her willing mouth.

Her breasts ached and her nipples drew into hard points. He fucked her mouth at a slow, leisurely pace. She tugged and squeezed his balls, eliciting more growling groans from him. Her clit throbbed and she became wetter and wetter as she continued to please him with her mouth.

He pulled back and drew her to her feet. "Enough." His fingers held a fine tremble where they gripped her upper arms. "I want to come inside you."

Sappy with the thought she'd brought him to the brink of his control, she grinned up at him. "Yes, please!" Then she wagged a finger. "But only if you do it hard and fast, like you promised."

"Don't forget desperate."

Her smile dimmed and her eyes heated. "I'd never forget desperate."

He shut off the water and haphazardly dried them, then swung her up in his arms and took her to Aodhán's bedroom. After laying her gently on her back, he slid her hips to the edge of the mattress and knelt at her feet. "Spread your legs."

She did as instructed, shivering. His big hands gripped her inner thighs and held her in place as he wedged his broad shoulders between her legs. The tip of his tongue flicked her clit, making her whimper and squirm. When he took a long, slow swipe with the flat of his tongue through the folds of her sex, she gasped and bucked against him, not sure if she wanted more or if it was too much.

"God, you're so wet. So slick." He put his mouth on her clit and suckled. She bit back a shriek and bucked her hips. A long finger slid inside her sheath, then another, stroking in and out. His lapping tongue and thrusting fingers catapulted her into ecstasy.

She was still quaking when he reared up over her. "Now," he said, his eyes glittering with silver fire, fangs curled over his bottom lip. "Now we get fast and hard."

"And desperate," she gasped.

He took his cock in his hand and positioned the head at the slick entrance to her body. His first hard thrust seated him to the balls. She moaned and grabbed his head, dragging his mouth down for a kiss. Lips ground together, tongues dueling. Against his mouth she said, "Be rough with me, Duncan. I need it rough."

He moaned at her entreaty. His hips jerked against hers hard and fast, just like he'd promised. Kimber was so aroused and wet that friction between their bodies instantly felt good. She lifted her hips to meet his thrusts and darted her tongue into his willing mouth. He gripped the comforter on either side of her head and snapped his hips. His cock plunged deep and with such force that she moaned in a frenzy of pleasure. She felt his heavy balls slap against the curve of her ass, and the suctioning sound of his cock plowing into her sheath drove her arousal ever higher.

When he lowered his body, their torsos touching now and mouths mating, every thrust of his groin against hers stimulated her clit. Their tongues dueled as he drove into her again and again.

"Duncan," she whispered against his cheek. Her thighs tensed as that fluttery panic started low in her core. "More. Harder! Oh, God!" She climaxed then, her whole body undulating beneath his larger frame. Duncan thrust so deep and hard she slid up the bed a few inches. His mouth settled over her throat and the pierce of his fangs sent her into another climax. He jerked roughly, his seed spilling into her. When he relaxed, he stayed buried deep inside her.

A few minutes later he rolled onto his back and pulled her against his side. "I knew it would be like that," he said softly, his voice deep and scratchy.

"Like what?" She traced an idle pattern against the hair-roughened skin of his chest.

"Amazing."

She smiled. It had been amazing. Life-affirming, even. Then she realized…

She bolted upright, clapping a hand on her neck. "You bit me."

His eyes narrowed. "Kimber, I'm a vampire. Vampires bite. You know this." When she didn't immediately respond, his eyes narrowed a little more. "You knew it when you told me to take you."

She clenched her jaw and moved away from him, suddenly and vulnerably aware of her nudity. He, however, seemed unconcerned about his as he leaned up on one elbow. "Kimber—"

She held up a hand. "Don't. Just…" She sighed. "Don't. I asked for it, Duncan. I wanted it." She fought to keep from hiding her pertinent bits with her hands. He'd already seen much more of her than he saw now. For God's sake, just a few minutes ago he'd been face first in her pussy. She knew it was a little late for modesty. "But you and I…" She shook her head. "I can't do this with you again. I'm sorry. I just can't."

She left the room before he could respond. She wasn't even sure what else she could say. After the first shock of Bishop's death had faded and her desperation to remind herself that she at least was still alive, the fear she had of vampires was back in full force. What if he hadn't stopped when he had? He could have drained her dry.

She eased into her room and pulled on a sweatshirt and shorts, and climbed into the twin bed that hugged the wall across from Natalie's.

"So you and Duncan finally did the deed?" Natalie's voice was soft in the darkness. When Kimber didn't reply, she added, "You tried to be quiet, but, well, it's not like this place is sound-proofed."

"I don't want to talk about it."

"Oh, it was that good, huh?" Natalie gave a soft snort of laughter.

"Shut up, Nat." Kimber rolled to her side, putting her back to her friend. In spite of her whirling thoughts, the events of the day caught up with her, and she sank into sleep.

* * *

An hour after Kimber left him, Duncan surged out of bed with a muttered curse. He grabbed a pair of Aodhán's sweats and yanked them on. Damn it, he should have paid attention to his gut. Kimber hadn't been ready to make love with him. She had a thing about being bitten, and he was a vampire. One who most certainly bit. Instead of focusing on his cock he should've been paying attention to what had happened to Bishop and how she was dealing with it.

He opened the bedroom door and stalked down the hallway to the living room. Throwing himself into the recliner, he tapped his fingers on the padded arm. Could he have made a bigger mess of things? Probably not.

Instead of making love to her, he should have made her talk about what she was feeling. But he'd led with his cock and allowed her to hide behind sex.

He scrubbed a hand over his face. Fuck. Shit. Damn it to hell.

Sitting around with only his maudlin thoughts for company wasn't something he particularly wanted to do. He realized the men that Bishop shared an apartment with, his former colleagues, had no idea the man was dead. The least he could do was inform them.

He headed down to Bishop's apartment and knocked on the door. Telling the two men of Bishop's death took only a few seconds, even with Duncan expressing his sympathies, something neither human seemed to want to hear. All too soon Duncan was back at Kimber's, sitting on the plump armchair, staring out at nothing in the darkened room. His glance caught the women's shoes, lying in front of the sofa where they'd kicked them off earlier. With a soundless sigh he stood and went over to pick them up. He lined them up against the wall by the door, where he'd already stashed his boots.

A low whimper sounded from the women's bedroom. He went still, listening. Another moan, and he jumped to his feet. He was inside the room in two seconds, just in time to clap his hand over Kimber's mouth as she surged up in bed with a scream. She struggled against him, tears wetting his fingers.

"Kimber, wake up." He gave her a shake. "You're dreaming. Wake up."

She gasped beneath his hand, her eyes flying open. He knew in the darkened room she couldn't see him, but he could see her just fine. Her hands grasped his shoulders and awareness flooded her eyes. He took his hand from her mouth.

"Duncan."

"I'm right here, sweetheart. You were dreaming."

She turned her face into his chest, her arms creeping around his back. "Something dark, shadowy reached for me and I couldn't get away. It was almost like I *wanted* it to have me. Bishop was there, too, but he was a zombie." She stifled a sob against him.

His chest hollowed. He might be able to protect her against zombies and his fellow vampires, but how could he protect her against her own mind? Feeling helpless, he put one hand to the back of her head and held her. "I'm sorry. I'm so sorry."

They were silent for a few moments. Duncan glanced over at the other bed and saw Natalie was sitting up, looking their way. Knowing she had counted Bishop as a friend, too, he murmured, "Nat, come on over here."

She scurried over to sit beside Kimber, and Duncan slid an arm around Natalie's shoulders. The three of them sat there, holding each other, while Duncan let the women grieve.

Finally Kimber sniffed and pulled back. "I would have done the same thing," she whispered.

He frowned. "What?"

"If someone I knew had been trying to save Carson at the risk of their own life, I would have done what you did." She wiped her cheeks. "I don't blame you."

"But you did. Then, when it was happening, you did blame me."

"Yes." She touched his cheek, the one she'd slapped. "I'm sorry for hitting you."

He smiled and pressed a kiss into her palm. "You already apologized for it."

"Yeah, well, I'm still sorry, I guess." She scooted back from him and he let his arms fall to his sides.

"You all right now?" he asked, hoping she'd ask him to stay, knowing she wouldn't. He knew she didn't trust him, his vampire side. He wasn't sure what he could say or do beyond what he already had to make her see she had nothing to fear from him.

"Yes."

He rose from the bed and made his way to the door, stopping when she called his name. In spite of the caution he felt, knowing he shouldn't hope, he turned back toward her.

"Thank you," she whispered. And that was all.

"You can always count on me, Kimber." He turned back to see her and Natalie sitting together still, their heads leaning against each other. "Always." He left them then, pulling the door behind him, and went back to the living room.

Was this the way it would be for them? Her turning to him only when she couldn't cope with her emotions? Him comforting her, protecting her then ending up alone?

Chapter Seven

Sunday passed quietly, with Kimber doing her best to ignore Duncan. For reasons of his own, he let her. Every once in a while she caught his gaze on her and looked at him before he could glance away. Each time she could have sworn she saw such uncertainty in his eyes that she told herself she was imagining things. Duncan was one of the most assured beings on the planet. There was no way his confidence was shaken by lil' ol' her.

Natalie looked like a spectator at a ping-pong match, watching them both closely, her gaze going from one to the other. At one point she muttered something about a train wreck, but when Kimber pressed her about it, she just shook her head and went to the kitchen for a glass of water.

Kimber rose on Monday morning after a restless night. Thankfully she hadn't had any more nightmares, but sleep had been elusive just the same. She pulled on a bra and underwear, a clean pair of navy blue sweats and matching zip-up fleece jacket, then sat on the bed to yank on thick socks. So she wouldn't wake

Natalie, she closed the bedroom door quietly behind her. As she padded toward the kitchen, she heard the low tones of men's voices. Duncan and Aodhán sat in the living room, a couple of candles burning on the coffee table. When they saw her they stopped talking.

Duncan got to his feet. "Good morning, Kimber." His raspy voice held the memories of their intimacies the night before last.

She fought back a blush. "Good morning." She cleared her throat and looked at Aodhán. "I'm glad you're back. When did you get in?"

"About an hour ago."

Duncan said, "By the way, I told Bishop's roommates what happened." He paused. "Can I talk to you for a moment?"

She lifted her chin. "There's nothing really for us to talk about. I meant what I said." On some level she realized she wasn't being fair to him, but she couldn't help what she was feeling. A vampire was a vampire was a vampire. Every time she let him bite her she handed him the chance to end her life.

The corners of his mouth dipped into a frown. "I think I'll get some sleep then," was all he said. His somber gaze caught hers, the hint of sadness tugging at her emotions. He hesitated beside her as if he were going to say more, but then his mouth tightened and he went on to Aodhán's room.

Kimber waited until she heard the door close. "What were you two talking about?"

"He told me what happened."

She stiffened. Duncan didn't seem the type to kiss and tell. Before she could respond, Aodhán went on. "I'm sorry about

Bishop." The fey warrior walked up to her and drew her into his arms. His big hands stroked up and down her back.

She leaned into him, thankful for his comfort, wishing he was Duncan. She went rigid at the thought and pushed away from him. She couldn't go there. Not ever again. Duncan was a vampire, a hunter. She was prey. All it would take for him to kill her would be one moment's slip of his control. A few seconds of him succumbing to the blood lust that was never far below the surface.

She didn't want to die at the hands of a zombie, and she sure as hell didn't want to die at the fangs of a vampire, either. And, if she were honest with herself, she didn't want Duncan to face an eternity of guilt for killing her. She knew he would. If she believed anything about him, she believed he didn't want to hurt her.

"I'm sorry, Kimber. I know Bishop was a friend," Aodhán murmured.

She clenched her jaws against a fresh onslaught of emotions. "I'm all right," she muttered and went into the kitchen. She turned on the faucet and filled a pan, then set it on the camp stove to heat. "Do you want some tea?"

"No coffee?"

She shook her head. "We drank the last of it a couple of days ago. The day we went to Maddalene's." God, that had only been on Saturday. It seemed like much more time had lapsed. She rolled her shoulders. She felt old.

"I'll take a cup of tea." Aodhán's voice was low. He was still in the living room.

Kimber gave a nod. Within minutes she had two cups of steaming water, each with a tea bag steeping. She handed one cup to Aodhán and sat on the sofa, curling her legs beneath her. "I think this is probably the last use we'll get out of these."

"The tea bags?"

"Yep." She tugged on the string of the tea bag and dunked it in and out of the water. "I think we've already used them three times. Maybe four. I think you and I are just going to drink hot water, really."

"That's all right." He shifted in the arm chair and crossed one leg over the other, resting his ankle on his knee.

"So, how're your people doing? Still zombie free?" She couldn't keep the bitterness out of her voice. The fey were under no obligation to help humans, but the fact that they'd made no overtures at all still rankled. At the very least they could have sent more warriors like Aodhán to kill off the zombies so that the survivors wouldn't have such a hell of a life.

"Kimber…" He set his cup down on the side table. "You know how my people feel about humans."

She pressed her lips together. "Yeah, like we're just one step above pond scum. I know."

He shook his head. "It's not that bad."

"Isn't it?" She looked at Aodhán. "They've left us out here to die, Aodhán. I think they'd like to see humans die off."

He heaved a sigh. "They wouldn't. But they would like to see humans stop messing with magic they don't understand and can't control."

She felt faint. There it was. In spite of everything he'd ever said to her, he *did* blame her for the Outbreak. "So you *do* think it's my fault. If I hadn't lost control, then none of this would have happened."

"Don't put words in my mouth, *mo chara*." He dropped his foot to the floor and leaned forward, clasping his hands between his knees. "Whatever happened that night, however things got out of control, it wasn't your fault."

She stared down into her cup. The faint light from the candles glittered weakly on the steaming liquid. Her thoughts drifted from the overall zombie problem to one specific person. Bishop. She'd been so close to drawing out the Unseen from him, from turning the tide on his turning. It wouldn't have mattered much in the overall scheme of things, but for her, personally, it would have been a huge victory.

What if... She lightly chewed on the inside of her cheek while she thought. What if she could draw out the Unseen from an actual zombie? If she could do it, then she could find a way to do it on a larger scale. She had to try.

Kimber surged to her feet and set her mug on the coffee table. "I need a zombie, and you're going to help me get one."

Aodhán's brows drew low over his eyes. "You what? And no, I'm not."

"I need a zombie," she repeated, her voice hard. "And yes, you are."

"Give me one good reason why I should." He leaned back in his chair and folded his arms across his wide chest. Stubborn son of a bitch.

"Because your people have left us out here with our asses flapping in the wind." She ignored his scowl. Okay, maybe the first reason was a stretch. Aodhán's people may not be helping, but he was. She plunged ahead. "Because I need to fix this. Because of everyone I know, you're one of the only ones that can." She wasn't going to say that Duncan was the only other one she knew who could catch a zombie.

His shoulders moved with his heavy sigh. "The Outbreak wasn't your fault. You don't have to fix it."

"Even if it wasn't my fault," she said, and she was nowhere near ready to accept that it wasn't, "I'd still have to try. I'm a necromancer, Aodhán. If I have the ability to reanimate life using the Unseen, I should be able to force the Unseen back into itself to un-animate life, right?"

His lips twisted. "I don't think that's a word."

She grunted. "What're you? The grammar king? You know what I mean. If I could force the Unseen back into itself and prevent it from reanimating the dead."

"Fine. Explain it to me."

"I just did." She paced in front of the sofa. "I was close with Bishop. Really close. If I—"

"Duncan said you almost died."

She waved one hand. "He exaggerated."

"He said your heart stopped. Twice."

She remembered her heart pounding, stuttering, remembered seeing the floating sparks behind her eyelids. She knew what had happened, but she couldn't let it stop her. "You'll be there to stop me if it looks like it's going too far."

"No."

Kimber dropped to her knees beside his chair and looked up at him. "Aodhán, please. I'm begging you. Help me find a way to set things right."

His bright blue eyes narrowed on her. "I know what tapping into the Unseen does to you, Kimber. I've been around when you've had nightmares." He cupped her cheek in one broad palm. "Just a couple of days ago I watched you nearly die. I don't call many people 'friend.'" His mouth thinned. "I value your friendship, *mo chara*. I would hate to lose it to death."

She couldn't give up on this. "Please."

He stared at her in silence. Finally he gave an abrupt nod. "Fine. We'll try it."

She jumped to her feet and ran over to the door to grab her ankle boots. "Excellent!" She sat on the couch and shoved her feet into her footwear.

"For the record, I think this is a very bad idea."

One of the bedroom doors opened. Thinking it was Duncan, that he'd overheard her plan and was coming to put a stop to it, her breath skittered in her throat. When Natalie came shuffling into the room, a big yawn only partially hidden behind one small hand, Kimber gave a sigh of relief.

Natalie stopped and stared at her. "What're you up to?"

Kimber frowned. "Nothing."

"Uh-huh." Her friend went into the kitchen and put the pan, still with water in it, back on the camping stove and lit the burner. "You looked guilty." She pointed to Kimber's feet. "And you have your boots on."

Kimber decided to ignore that. "I need you to stay here and keep an eye on things. Duncan's sleeping."

Natalie put one hand on her hip and looked from Kimber to Aodhán and back again. "Why? Where are you two going?"

"I'll tell you later." No way in hell did she want Duncan waking up and finding out from Natalie what was going on. And he would find out. Natalie couldn't keep a secret to save her life.

"We won't be far," Aodhán said. He opened the door and looked at Natalie. "Lock this behind us."

"Oh, do you really think I should?" she asked, her voice rife with sarcasm. "I thought I'd leave it open and invite potential ravagers and looters to come in."

A growl of frustration rumbled up from deep in his chest.

"Not now, you two," Kimber muttered. She smacked him in the stomach with the back of her hand. "Come on."

Twenty minutes later they were in the basement of the apartment building, a somewhat fresh zombie attached with chains to one of the empty vending machines lining the hallway that led to the laundry facility. This shuffler looked like it had turned within the last few weeks. He didn't smell too bad, and his flesh, though mottled, hadn't started putrefying yet.

The zombie lunged for them, teeth snapping, arms reaching. Thankfully the vending machine was heavy enough that he couldn't get close enough.

"Just how are you going to do this?" Aodhán asked. He stroked his chin. "Whenever you reanimated a corpse, you had to touch them to direct the Unseen into the body, correct?"

She nodded. "Yes." She didn't want to get close enough to this thing to have to touch it, but she wasn't sure she had another option. "Can you chain his legs to the bottom of the machine? I can touch his ankle."

"If six months ago someone had told me I'd be into zombie bondage, I'd have punched him in the face." He heaved a sigh and set about lashing the zombie's ankles to the feet of the vending machine, this time using rope. "There. He's as secure as I can make him."

"Okay." Kimber drew a deep breath. "You stand where he can see you and keep his attention on you. Maybe he won't realize I'm down at his feet." She dropped to her knees and sidled forward slowly. The zombie kept its gaze on Aodhán, hands grasping in the air as the undead thing tried to get hold of the fey warrior.

With trembling fingers, she slipped her hand beneath the zombie's tattered slacks and rested her hand on his leg, just above where his sock had scrunched around his ankle. Closing her eyes, she focused inward, drawing on her ability to tap into the Unseen. After another moment or so she stretched out with her mind to the bit of the Unseen that animated the zombie. A few seconds ticked by and nothing happened. Then raw, black energy surged up, lunging for her just like it had all those months ago with Richard Whitcomb.

The zombie went crazy, jerking against his bindings, his mouth open, ferocious snarls coming from his throat. His teeth snapped together, the sound loud in the otherwise silent basement. She heard the rattle of chains, then a screech and a metallic moaning sound. It took a few seconds for her to realize the zombie was pulling free of his chains.

Just as Aodhán yelled her name, she scrambled away from the undead thing. The fey warrior pulled his sword and shoved the blade through the zombie's mouth with an upward thrust. He twisted the sword and pulled it free, leaving the lifeless shuffler dangling from his remaining bindings.

She sat on the floor, dragging in air, and tried to calm her thundering heart. The coolness of the concrete bled through the fabric of her sweatpants.

"Well," Aodhán said. He wasn't even out of breath. "That went well."

Kimber, on the other hand, had trouble gulping in enough air. She pushed to her feet. "It didn't go like I thought it would."

"Really? You actually thought this out?"

She glared at him. "Well, you could have said something." She was being unreasonable and she knew it, but crap! That zombie had almost had her for breakfast.

"I believe when I said 'This is a really bad idea' that *was* me saying something."

"Sorry." She stared at the zombie. "There's something wrong with the Unseen."

"What does that mean?" Aodhán came to her side. A quick glance at him showed her that his gaze, too, was on the zombie.

"At Whitcomb's animation, when I first tried to return him to true death, the Unseen reached for me. It was dark. Evil." She shivered anew at the memory. "Something other than Richard Whitcomb's soul attached to him."

"Like a stowaway?"

She nodded. "Or a parasite. But I don't know what it was. What it *is*."

"But you think that, whatever it is, it's what started the apocalypse?"

"Yes." She rubbed her palms down the front of her sweatpants. She gestured toward the wilted zombie. "We need to get this thing out of here."

He stared at her. "Promise me you won't try to do this again."

She met his gaze. "I don't think I can promise that, Aodhán. I need to figure something out, and I can only do that by trying."

"And failing."

"Hey, three-quarters of the world's inventions came about through failures, you know. Edison tried like ten thousand times until he finally got the light bulb to function properly. At least I'll know what doesn't work."

He shook his head. "You promise me, or I'll tell Duncan what you did here today."

She widened her eyes. "Are you serious? You're gonna run and tell Dad?"

"I hardly think you look on him as a father figure, and I know he sure as hell doesn't think of you as a daughter." He folded his arms and broadened his stance. "But I'm very serious, Kimber. This is too dangerous, messing with the Unseen this way. You saw what happened with this one. You made it stronger. Worse. Imagine if that happened with a horde. Or all of them."

He was right. They'd never survive if zombies got any stronger than they already were. But she couldn't stand by and do nothing. She had to keep trying, and if that meant lying to Aodhán, then so be it.

"Fine." She made sure her voice was less than gracious. "I promise." She crossed her fingers behind her back. If he could be childish enough to threaten to tattle on her, she could be childish enough to believe her promise was negated by the simple act of putting one finger over the other.

The Outbreak was her fault, and she would find a way to fix it.

Chapter Eight

Two nights later Duncan answered the knock on Kimber's door. Murray stood there, just as fragile looking as ever. "What now?" Duncan asked.

The other vampire lifted his chin, motioning toward the inside of the apartment. "Maddalene wants to see your little necromancer again." His face was expressionless but Duncan caught the smirk in his voice.

He clenched his jaw. No way in hell was Kimber going back there until he and Maddalene came to an understanding. The fact that Maddalene had overridden him and allowed hungry vampires into his living quarters, to threaten Kimber and her friends, had driven home the point that the sense of loyalty he felt toward Maddalene was a one-way street.

"Tell Maddalene to forget it," he told Murray.

"I'm not your messenger boy, MacDonnough." The skinny excuse for a vampire gave a grunt and pointed to his head. "Still attached, the way I like it. You got something to say to Maddalene, you say it yourself." He gave a sardonic salute with two fingers and sauntered off.

Damn it.

Duncan closed the door and turned to face the other inhabitants of the apartment. Natalie stood in the kitchen, leaning back against the counter, her hands braced on either side. Aodhán was kicked back in the recliner, his gaze steady and calm. Kimber, his lovely Kimber, stood beside the sofa, arms crossed and one foot tapping on the floor.

"I am not going back there," she said.

"No, you're not."

"I mean it, Duncan. Maddalene wants the impossible, and I won't do it."

"I agree."

"No matter what you…" A frown dipped between her brows. "Wait. What?"

He couldn't stop the small grin that quirked his lips. She was adorable when she was confused. It wasn't a look he got to see very often because she had such a sharp mind. "I said I agree. You're not going to see Maddalene."

"Oh." Her hands dropped to her sides. "Um, why not?"

Ignoring the interested gazes of Aodhán and Natalie, he walked over to Kimber and took her face in his palms. "Because I don't trust her right now, and I mean to keep you safe."

Her lips parted and he couldn't stop himself from dipping his head to press a soft kiss against her mouth. When he drew away, her lashes fluttered and swept up to show slightly dazed eyes. That was a good sign, anyway. He knew she wasn't indifferent to him. If he could prove to her that he wouldn't lose control and drain her, maybe one day she'd trust him enough to let him close again. To let him love her.

He took a step back. Where the hell had that come from? He didn't love Kimber. He couldn't love her. She was mortal. He was not. He didn't deny he wanted her—his lust for her was nearly a living entity on its own. But love?

No.

He didn't have the time for love. He didn't have the luxury for love.

He didn't have the right. He'd done things he wasn't proud of. Kimber deserved better than him. She certainly didn't deserve the danger he'd be putting her in if Maddalene found out he had a soft spot for Kimber. And he deserved…

He firmed his jaw. He deserved only what she gave him. But that didn't negate the fact that she had something he wanted—well, actually, two things he wanted: the ability to contact the Unseen and a body he wanted to lose himself in. Both might be within his reach if he could just get Maddalene to back the hell off.

Yeah, Duncan. Just keep telling yourself all you're interested in is her body. You might really believe it someday.

He turned away from Kimber. Grabbing up the tire iron from where he'd placed it underneath the coffee table, he headed toward the front door. "I'm going to talk to Maddalene."

"Wait." Kimber's soft voice stopped him. When he looked over his shoulder at her, she said, "Be careful."

He gave a nod and pulled open the door. As he closed it behind him, he heard Aodhán say, "He's strong and he's fast. On his own, he'll be able to get around any zombies out there. He'll be fine."

Fine against zombies, yes. Against his own heart? He wasn't so sure.

* * *

Half an hour later Duncan stood in front of Maddalene, watching her eyes flare with rage. Her two human attendants, clad only in black bikini briefs, knelt at either end of the chaise. Dried blood streaked their inner forearms and the strong muscles of their throats. Four well-fed vampire guards stood in front of the closed door, blocking the exit. Even as strong as he was, Duncan wasn't a match for guards who'd recently fed.

"Repeat what you just said to me, Duncan," Maddalene said, her voice dangerously soft. "I think I must have misheard you."

"You didn't mishear anything. I told you to leave Kimber alone. She's fragile right now. She just lost a friend." He maintained eye contact with her, refusing to look away and show weakness. "With the Outbreak, everything's changed. Everyone's fighting to survive. What you want Kimber to do for you doesn't matter anymore."

"What I want doesn't matter?" She rose from her chaise and glided down the steps. She wore form-fitting black leggings and a dark purple top that fell off one slim shoulder. Her long hair fell in loose curls over her shoulders. For all that she was a beautiful woman, he never forgot that she could be deadly. "You forget yourself. What I want is all that matters."

He clenched his jaw so tight the muscles in his jaw flexed. Calling upon all his reserves of diplomacy, he said softly, "At what cost, my queen?"

Her full lips thinned. "And you're the one to determine the cost?" She slashed a slim hand through the air, forestalling his reply. Her dark eyes glittered with emotion. If he hadn't known her as well as he did, he might have thought she battled back tears. She flipped her hair over her shoulder with a quick flick of her elegant fingers. "You know how much Eduardo means to me. How can that not matter?"

"It's not worth the havoc you may wreak trying to revive him." As she stopped in front of him, he lifted his hands and placed them lightly on her shoulders. Had he been anyone other than her second in command he would never have dared be so familiar. "Maddalene, listen to me, please. Kimber has said there's something wrong with the Unseen, and I believe her. When her friend Bishop was bitten, she tried to draw the infection—that part of the Unseen that is powering these undead things—out of him, and it nearly killed her. What you ask is too much."

Her nostrils flared. "Who are you to defy me?"

He gave her a little shake. "I'm your friend, damn it. Believe it or not, I am trying to help you." He needed her to believe that. If she suspected his only motivation was to keep Kimber safe, Maddalene would never agree to leave her alone.

"Are you?" She knocked his hands away and took a few steps back. "I think you're less concerned about me than you are about your little human. Has she let you fuck her yet?" His answer must have shown on his face, because she trilled a laugh. "Oh, I see she has. And it has strengthened your noble desire to protect her."

"Even if Kimber and I hadn't become intimate," Duncan said, "I would still counsel you against this action. Maddalene, it can't be done."

With a flick of her wrist she summoned the guards. Duncan allowed two of them to take his arms in their hold. The only thing he'd accomplish by fighting them would be to use strength he might need later. "What is this?" he asked.

"I cannot allow disobedience and treachery in my own enclave." She grabbed the neckline of his T-shirt and with preternatural strength ripped it down the front. She brushed the ruined material aside, baring his chest and stomach. "The disloyalty you have demonstrated must be answered."

She walked behind him and ripped at his shirt until it was in tatters. She pulled it off him, leaving him naked from the waist up.

"Since when is it disloyal to counsel you against taking action I believe to be unwise?" Duncan kept his voice even, though anger simmered below the surface. If she thought to intimidate him, she could think again. "I've done it before. And I'll do it again."

"Yet you've always bowed to my wishes in the end. Except now. Why?" She studied him, her eyes steady on his. "Why now? Why her?" Those dark eyes widened. "You have feelings for her."

To admit he cared for Kimber would put her in more danger than she already was. He wouldn't give Maddalene anything more to hold over his head to force his compliance. Enough was enough. "No," he denied, keeping his voice as even as the gaze he leveled on his queen. "She is a means to an end."

"What end?" Her suspicious eyes remained fixed on him.

He debated telling her, and decided he wouldn't get anywhere by remaining silent. As much as he didn't want to bare his soul, if he even still had one, in front of her guards, he didn't have much of a choice at the moment. "We've often wondered if the Unseen is what makes us what we are," he began.

She nodded. "Yes. If necromancers can use it to reanimate corpses into zombies, perhaps that same essence is what allows vampires to exist."

Nerves dried his mouth. If she didn't believe him, or didn't care, he knew she would take out her anger at his defiance on his body. Like he'd told Kimber before, she was a cruel and harsh mistress. "I want…" He drew in a reflexive breath, a holdover from those long ago days as a human when extra oxygen could somehow lend extra resolve. "I need to feel again, Maddalene. I need…to feel a connection to the living."

"So get a dog."

Irritation roiled through him at her flippant response. "Maddalene…"

She jerked one shoulder up, an unspoken acknowledgment and apology over her trivialization of his heartfelt desire. "This is important to you."

"Yes."

Her hard gaze drifted over his face and lower, to his chest. "As is my dream of being reunited with Eduardo."

He could tell by the unforgiving expression on her face that she had set aside any sense of being in the wrong and was putting her desires above his. It was her right as queen, though a truly worthy leader would look to the betterment of her people over the fulfillment of her own hopes. But Maddalene had always been a selfish ruler.

She threw one arm behind her and clicked her fingers. "Bring chains and the cat o' nine tails."

One of her human attendants jumped to his feet and hurried toward the back wall where a number of whips and chains complete with manacles were stored. After he grabbed the requested implements, he rushed to her side and placed the handle of the whip in her outstretched hand. The bits of glass attached at the ends of the lashes glinted in the artificial light of the room.

Duncan stared at them and then looked at his queen. She had never looked as regal and ruthless as she did now. He was fucked, and everyone in the room knew it. If he fought, he might win and get out of the room, but there were dozens of vamps he'd have to battle to get out of the building. He was strong.

But he wasn't that strong.

Besides, if he allowed Maddalene to work out her frustrations on him, she might be more inclined to leave Kimber alone. For a while, anyway. And, also, he wasn't ready to play his hand just yet. He'd known for a while that her time to rule needed to end, but he'd been resistant to doing anything about it because of his loyalty. Their friendship. And yet, if she was willing to stripe his back, to mangle it with a cat o' nine tails, then it was clear to him their friendship was one-sided.

The human handed over the chains to one of the guards standing behind Duncan.

Maddalene pointed toward the central supporting column in the room. "Chain him securely," she instructed the guards.

They dragged him to the column. Duncan again thought about fighting, and the muscles of his arms and legs tightened as he prepared to jerk the two holding him toward each other to throw them off balance. He forced himself to relax and looked over his shoulder at Maddalene. "I want your word you'll leave Kimber alone."

She raised one arched eyebrow. "And why would I do that?"

He held her gaze. "What you're about to do is because of anger, not because it's just. And you know it." But he'd let her do it, because it would be an outlet for her frustration. He'd rather be used as her whipping boy than have Kimber be the recipient of Maddalene's vitriolic attitude.

Her nostrils flared. Fists clenched at her sides, the knuckles of her right hand showing white around the handle of the whip, she stalked forward. The closer she got, the more he could smell the scorched rubber scent of her anger. She placed the tip of the handle under his chin, forcing his head back so that he had to look down his nose to meet her eyes. Silver glinted in the brown of her irises. "I will give you twenty lashes for your disloyalty," she said. "Keep trying my patience and it will be forty."

He turned his head and rested his cheek against the column. "After all this time, I would have thought you'd have more faith in me," he murmured.

"Forty it is." Her voice struck like flint in his ear, her breath stirring his hair. "Ask Aodhán some time about how I feel about betraying males." Before he could question her about that, she stepped away from him.

The guards snapped the manacles around his wrists and attached the other ends to rings high up on the column, forcing Duncan to his toes. They moved away from him and waited in silence.

The first slice of the lashes across his back startled him with the amount of pain. He ground his jaw, determined to take his unfair punishment in silence. By the tenth lash he couldn't hold back the moans. By the thirtieth, feeling like his back was so much shredded meat, each strike of the individual lashes brought screams to his throat. By the final stroke he sagged against the chains holding him to the column.

"Release him." Maddalene's voice came to him through a fog of pain. If the guards on either side of him hadn't grasped his arms, he would have collapsed to the floor in a heap of misery. Still seeming far away, his queen ordered, "He does not feed for forty-eight hours. Understand? He will bear scars for his disloyalty."

"Yes, my queen."

She grasped his hair and pulled his head up. He stared up at her, pain and biting betrayal swirling through him. "I. Want. The. Necromancer. She will be more willing if you convince her." She gave his head a shake. "Submit to me, Duncan, and we can be as we were. Hold to your stubbornness, and you'll be in chains feeling the bite of that whip again." She let go of his hair, and his head slumped to his chest. "Take him."

The guards dragged Duncan out of the room and down the hallway to his own suite. Instead of dumping him on the floor in the living room, as he expected, they took him into his bedroom and placed him face down on the bed.

He was aware when they left but then floated in a haze of muddled pain and anger. Even hatred of Maddalene, which was new. But then she'd never before taken the cat to his back, though he'd seen it done often enough to others.

The air held the coppery scent of his blood and the dark spice of his pain. He lay there in a daze, his back on fire, his entire body aching from the tension he'd held in his muscles.

The outer door opened and closed then footsteps sounded on the carpet. "Well, my friend," a man's raspy voice muttered. "You've really done it this time."

Duncan let loose a bark of laughter, then groaned when even that movement hurt. "Atticus. Have you come to commiserate or condemn?"

A blessedly cool, wet cloth draped across his lacerated back, bringing a small measure of relief.

"Commiserate then," Duncan murmured.

His friend went down on his haunches beside the bed and balanced by placing one hand on the top of the mattress. A haze of pain made it hard for Duncan to focus on his friend. He blinked, bringing the face of the former gladiator into focus.

"We've been instructed to stay away from you for two days," Atticus said.

"So you're here because…?"

Atticus grinned. "I never have been able to take orders." His face sobered and he shook his head. "What the hell was this all about?"

Duncan closed his eyes. "She wants Kimber to raise Eduardo."

Atticus was silent a moment. "She must hope your necromancer will have success where others have failed."

Duncan's eyes flew open. "What? She's tried before?"

"Six months ago. The necromancer failed and lost his life in the attempt."

"I didn't know." He frowned. Agony streaked through the damaged nerves in his back and at the renewed sense of betrayal at his queen's hands.

"And she obviously still wishes to try."

With a slight snort, Duncan looked at his friend. "I've been telling her for six months to give it up, but she won't. Tonight she decided to 'punish' me for my disloyalty."

A frown furrowed a deep line between Atticus's eyebrows. "How exactly have you been disloyal?"

"By protecting Kimber instead of helping Maddalene coerce her into something I don't think she can do. And even if Kimber could do what Maddalene wants, I don't think she'd survive it."

"And her survival is important to you." It was a statement, not a question.

"Yes." Fatigue and sharp stabs of pain ate at his consciousness. He closed his eyes again. "You know where she lives. I need you to get word to Aodhán that I'll be...delayed." He stared at Atticus. "Don't let Kimber know what happened. She'll worry."

Atticus rolled his eyes and stood. "And you think your fairy friend won't?" When Duncan tried to lever himself up on his elbows, Atticus put a gentle hand on his shoulder. "Be at ease, my friend. It will be as you wish." He shook his head. "I'll send a messenger and come back to clean your back and put some ointment on it. It's all I can do at the moment." He paused. "Maddalene leaves in a few hours for a meeting with one of the queens in the southern part of the state. She should be gone several days. I'll do more as soon as she's left the premises."

Duncan let his eyelids fall closed once more. "I didn't expect what you've done already, so thank you." He felt his grip on consciousness begin to ravel apart. The last thing he heard was Atticus's raspy voice as he spoke with someone else. Duncan's head whirled. He stopped fighting the allure of darkness and slipped into the arms of oblivion.

Chapter Nine

After a night spent tossing and turning, listening for Duncan's return and never hearing it, Kimber rolled out of bed. Thrusting her arms through her ratty purple terrycloth robe, she wandered out into the main area and saw Aodhán standing in front of the kitchen sink, dressed in his usual cotton T-shirt and jeans. "Didn't Duncan ever come back?" she asked him.

He turned his back and placed his mug in the sink. "He sent a message that he's been delayed. He'll be back in a few days."

"A few *days*?" Kimber moved to stand beside Aodhán. There was something wrong, she could tell. He wouldn't meet her eyes. The way he shifted his weight on his feet demonstrated his discomfort with a conversation that had just begun. "What happened?" she asked. "What's going on?"

"What's going on is that both of you have asked me to keep secrets, and I'm tired of it." He faced her, leaning his hip against the counter. "I'll tell you what happened to Duncan as long as you understand that the first opportunity I get I'll also tell him about your zombie experiment."

Her breath hitched in her throat. For him to threaten to divulge a confidence was…well, a huge deal. Once his word was given, Aodhán didn't go back on it. It was a matter of personal honor. Something horrible had happened to Duncan. That was the only explanation for Aodhán now being so willing to break a confidence.

"Tell me," she whispered.

"Two hours ago a vampire messenger sent by a friend of Duncan's told me that Maddalene had Duncan…" His mouth pursed in a grimace of distaste. "She had him punished."

"Punished how?" A pulse pounded at the side of her neck, and she pressed her fingers to it as if she could control it somehow.

"Forty lashes with a cat o' nine tails that has shards of glass embedded in the strands."

As realization of the damage that would do struck home, her eyes widened. Her mouth dried. "Oh, my God." Feeling sick to her stomach, she wrapped her arms around her waist. *Duncan.* "Why?"

"Why do you think?" His eyes narrowed and for the first time she saw censure in their sky-blue depths. "He was protecting you. As always. Yet you credit him with nothing. Thank him for nothing. Give him nothing." His voice never lost its calm displeasure. "And blame him for everything."

"That's not true!" Kimber pushed away from the counter and stalked into the living room. "Well, maybe I did, in the past. But I've changed my mind." She caught herself and qualified, "I did sort of blame him for Bishop, but that was in the heat of the moment, in anger. I apologized later. I know there was no choice, and it was what Bishop wanted." She tightened her arms around her middle. "And I've thanked him plenty."

God in heaven, she sounded as sulky and sullen as a teenager.

"Have you really? Perhaps with pretty words you've thanked him, and if it were anyone other than Duncan that might suffice. But he needs more than pretty words from you." When she would have responded, he lifted one hand. "And you know it."

"But we..." She clamped her lips together, not ready to divulge intimate details of her relationship with Duncan. It was complicated. She drew in a breath and forced herself to look inward. Had she made it more complicated than it needed to be? Was she truly scared of Duncan?

Or was she scared of what he made her feel? Lust, certainly. Anxious, absolutely. But fear?

It was time to face the truth. She'd never been frightened of Duncan. Ever.

She closed her eyes, tears burning behind the lids. Even before the Outbreak he'd looked out for her, and *that* was when she'd started running scared. Vampires had always spooked her and she'd used that fear to hold Duncan at arms' length. It wasn't well done of her at all.

Pinching the bridge of her nose, she rotated her shoulders to work out some of the tension building there. "How badly is he hurt?" she asked quietly.

"There were glass shards embedded in the leather of the whip, Kimber." Aodhán's voice was hushed with distress. "His back is in shreds, and he's been forbidden to feed for two days."

She stared at him in horror. "So he won't be able to heal his

back right away?" She clenched her fists. If he didn't get a fresh
infusion of blood soon after being injured, he'd be left with horrible scars. "She *wants* him scarred."

Aodhán gave an abrupt nod. "Aye. In her eyes he's chosen you
over her. She would have given him only twenty lashes for that,
but when he pressed her on the issue she added another twenty.
She means for him to wear his marks of dishonor."

Well, this situation was completely unacceptable. She wasn't
going to allow Duncan to suffer for his protection of her. If that
meant facing down the bitch on her own turf, so be it.

"Give me a minute to get dressed and get something to eat,
and we'll go." She turned toward the bedroom.

"Are you certain you want to do this?"

She looked over her shoulder at the fey warrior. "I don't have
a choice, Aodhán. He's in pain because of me. If you help me get
past the vampires between him and me, I can help him."

"As always, I am at your service." His lips curled in a slow,
wicked grin. "Especially against Maddalene and her blood suck-
ers."

When she went back into the bedroom, Kimber roused
Natalie and explained what was going on. Natalie jumped up and
threw on her clothes. "I'm going, too," she said.

"You don't have to," Kimber said. She slid her hatchet through
one of her belt loops. "I don't know how many of the vamps are
loyal enough to Duncan to let us through."

"Doesn't matter." Natalie took Kimber's hands in hers and
gave her fingers a squeeze. "Duncan's been here for us over the last
six months. He's saved our lives more than once. If there's something we can do for him, we have to."

Kimber pulled Natalie into a hug. "Thank you," she whispered. "I love you, you know that, right?"

Her friend patted her on the back and drew back. "I love you more." Her grin was quick and easy, but Kimber caught the shine of tears in her eyes.

"I should say it more often," Kimber murmured.

Natalie grabbed up her short sword. "I know how you feel, hon. No worries." She slipped the sword into the scabbard she'd attached to her thigh. "Let's go kick some vampire butt."

An hour later, Kimber felt a vague sense of disquiet. She, Natalie and Aodhán stood at the gates to Maddalene's complex. They'd gotten here with relative ease, having had to dispatch only three zombies. For once she'd managed to do it without getting any goo on herself, as had her friends. So when the vampire guards at the gates allowed them entrance, she frowned. It all seemed a little too easy.

"Have the stars aligned in our favor or something?" Natalie whispered.

"That's what I was just thinking," Kimber responded quietly. She kept a tight grip on the hatchet, though, just in case they were being lulled into a false sense of security. She wouldn't put it past the rat bastards. Vampires were a tricky bunch.

When they entered the lobby of the enclave, a tall brute of a man stood waiting for them. He had to have been at least six-five, broad shouldered and lean hipped. As she got closer she realized his irises were vampire silver, though he seemed calm enough. She'd heard that once vamps hit a certain age—something around a thousand years or so—their eyes went silver and stayed there. So this guy was *old*. His hair was so black it seemed to absorb light and rioted in short curls surrounding a face that, had it been even a fraction less masculine, would have been called beautiful. Feminine, even. But sensually cruel lips and a sharp blade of a nose lent strength to his face. The thin scar that bisected his left cheek also kept him from being too pretty.

He nodded to Aodhán and looked from Kimber to Natalie. "Miss Treat?"

She lifted one hand. "I'm Kimberly Treat."

He perused her, his face expressionless. She couldn't tell if he was impressed or found her wanting, and gave herself a mental kick for even caring.

"We'd like to see Duncan. Please." Even though she wanted to rail at him and demand he take her to Duncan *right now*, she figured good manners wouldn't hurt. Might even help.

"I am Marcus Atticus. You may call me Atticus. I'm Maddalene's third."

Kimber blinked. "Sorry, her third?"

Those otherworldly eyes didn't waver. "Third in command, following Duncan. If he's not here or is…unavailable, I'm in charge. When you arrived at the gates seeking entrance, since Maddalene is not on site and Duncan is…indisposed, the guards contacted me."

"I see." Just how badly injured was Duncan? "Please, I need to see him."

Atticus inclined his head and with a rather knightly flourish swept out an arm. "This way."

"After you," she murmured.

His lips twitched but he obligingly turned toward the stairs. He led them up to Duncan's door and opened it. Once they'd all filed inside, he closed the door and moved to the middle of the room. As before, a fire burned in the living room fireplace, and Kimber noticed an additional scent—cinnamon and cloves.

Atticus stood at attention, his hands clasped behind his back. With his broad shoulders straight, his legs spread, he looked…dangerous. And really sexy, but she felt no draw toward him other than the natural feminine appreciation of a good-looking man. Now he said, "I will keep news of your presence at the enclave as quiet as I can for as long as I can, but you must realize that sooner rather than later Maddalene will learn you're here. The fragrance bark I put in the fire will mask your scent for the time being. Once she returns from her visit with one of the queens in the southern part of the state, I'll make certain her attention is directed elsewhere for a few days, but I can't promise more than that." He motioned toward the bedroom. "Help him while you can." As he opened the door to the hallway, he said, "I'll have two friends stand guard, those I know are loyal to me rather than our queen." Then he was gone.

Kimber went into the bedroom, aware but not really paying attention as Natalie and Aodhán followed her. She went straight to the bed where Duncan lay on his stomach. The sight of his back, skin hanging loose in shreds and even missing in large patches, made bile rise in her throat. She heard Natalie gag, and Aodhán's quiet suggestion that she wait in the other room.

"Oh, Duncan." Kimber went to her knees beside the bed and stroked her hand gently over his cheek.

His eyes opened, the brilliant green dulled with pain. "Kimber?" Confusion drew down his brows. "What're you doing here?"

"We came as soon as Aodhán told me what happened."

Duncan's scowl bounced off the fey warrior. "He wasn't supposed to tell anyone."

"Yes, well, he's gonna tattle on me, too, so don't get too upset." She glanced at his back again and couldn't hold back the tears. "Duncan, why? Why would she do this to you?"

"She demands absolute obedience." This came from Aodhán. "And throws a temper tantrum like a child when she doesn't get it." He gave a snort. "And this one is so pigheaded about the debt he supposedly owes her that he has stayed decades too long."

Duncan shifted against the bed. A low groan dragged from his throat. There was one thing Kimber could do for him, and by God she would do it. She owed him.

She shrugged out of her denim jacket and let it fall to the floor, then pushed up the sleeve of her bright yellow sweatshirt. Thrusting her wrist in front of his mouth, she said, "Here."

"What are you doing?" He pulled his head back, putting a few more inches between her wrist and his lips.

"You won't heal if you don't feed. And if you wait much longer to feed, you'll heal with scars." She moved her wrist closer. "Bite me. And this time I mean it."

* * *

"Why are you doing this?" Duncan stared at Kimber's face, forcing himself with every bit of control he had to not look at the blue-veined wrist plunked beneath his nose. This close he could smell the salty scent of perspiration mixed with the lighter floral aroma of her body wash. The flowery notes were faded, not fresh, so he knew her shower must have been last night. That thought brought the memory of being in the shower with her to the forefront of his mind, and blood surging to his cock brought that part of his anatomy forefront as well.

"Bite me, Duncan," Kimber said again. "You need this."

He shook his head. "You don't want me to bite you. You said—"

"Forget what I said before. I was an idiot." She brought her other hand up and brushed his hair away from his face. "Duncan, you're the only vampire here who can protect us." She made a face. "That makes me sound pretty mercenary, doesn't it? I want you to get better. I need you."

As the realization of exactly what was going on hit him, alarm flared. She was here. At Maddalene's conclave. The headstrong, impetuous…"You're right. You are an idiot. What were you thinking, coming here?" He pushed up, gritting his teeth against the pain in his back, and swung his legs over the edge of the bed.

She stood. "I was thinking I could help you, you stubborn ass." Once again that slender, frail wrist was thrust beneath his nose. "Bite."

He shook his head. "No. Atticus will protect you."

"Oh, for fuck's sake." She dropped her arm to her side and clenched her fists. "As much as it hurts my inner feminist to admit this, I do need the protection. Against one vamp I might be able to hold my own. Maybe. But against an entire enclave? Probably not. Atticus said he'd make sure Maddalene was distracted for a few days. Anyway, I'll feel a hell of a lot better if Atticus, Aodhán *and* you protect us." She shoved her arm up again, bumping his nose with the fleshy part of her palm.

Before he could tell her to get away from him, he heard Aodhán's deep voice. "She's right, Duncan. We need you at full strength, especially now that Kimber and Natalie are here." He moved to stand closer. "I'll make sure you stop in time, if that's what's worrying you."

"It's what's always worried *her*." He nodded toward Kimber.

"Well, then, I'll be here to set both of you at ease."

Kimber blew out a breath, her exasperation clear to see. "Duncan, for crying out loud. Just. Bite. Me."

He couldn't fight it any longer. His fangs elongated. His eyes burned, and he let the feral part of him come out. He licked across the silken skin of her inner wrist, then, holding onto her arm with gentle hands, bit down into her tender flesh.

Her hot blood slid down his throat, nourishing him, enticing him. Seducing him. Even as he felt his body begin to heal, his cock hardened. After a few seconds, he retracted his fangs and licked across the puncture wounds in her wrist. He looked down at her. At some point during his feeding she'd gone to her knees and now knelt between his legs. She glanced at his erection then met his gaze, her own eyes dark, the pupils dilated.

"All right, then," Aodhán murmured. "I'll just go back out into the living room with Natalie. Oh, by the way, your friend Atticus said he put two of his friends on your door and will do his best to keep Maddalene from finding out Kimber's here as long as he can."

"Thanks," Duncan said without looking away from Kimber. He stood, drawing Kimber to her feet, and waited until the door closed behind his fey friend before he reached out to tuck her hair behind her ear, letting his hand linger near her cheek. "And thank you, too. I know this was hard for you."

She licked her lips, leaving shiny, tantalizing moisture behind. "Not as hard as it was for you," she replied with another glance at his groin.

He gave a bark of laughter. Leave it up to his Kimber to find humor in the situation.

He stilled. His Kimber. *His*. With a smothered oath, he cradled her head in his hands and leaned forward, slanting his mouth over hers with pent-up, desperate desire.

Chapter Ten

Kimber drew back from Duncan with a gasp. "Wait!"

His face settled into grim lines. He dropped his hands to his sides and took a step away from her. "I'm sorry." His voice was as stiff as she'd ever heard it. "I thought…"

He'd misunderstood. She hadn't pulled back because she didn't want him. "Duncan, stop. I just…" When he wouldn't look at her, she sighed and put one hand on his cheek. He let her tilt his face toward her but his gaze remained fixed above her head. "I want you." At his skeptical look she insisted, "I do. Really, I do. But your back…"

He twisted. She gasped again, this time with disbelief. His back wasn't completely healed, but it was no longer the bloody, raw mess it had been earlier. The skin was pink and looked like it would still be sensitive, but it had knitted together.

"Well, then," she murmured. He turned around to face her again and she gave his shoulders a gentle push. He obligingly sat on the bed. "Can you put pressure on your back?" she asked.

He moved, settling his back against the pillows propped against the solid cherry headboard. Not one flicker of pain crossed his face or moved through his eyes. Silently she pulled her sweatshirt over her head, letting him get a look at her breasts confined in a lacy black bra. She toed off her shoes and shimmied out of her jeans, and wished her panties were as sexy as her bra. But, no, she'd gone for comfort and so had cotton granny panties on. The flare in his eyes told her that didn't matter to him.

With a smile she got back on the bed on her knees, kneeling at his hip, and leaned forward, bracing herself with one hand gripping the headboard. She placed a soft kiss against his mouth, gave his bottom lip a sharp nip and then laved away the sting with her tongue. Another kiss to the corner of his eye, his nose, beside his ear.

She would show him with her mouth, her hands, her body, that she acknowledged what was between them.

Her kisses wandered across his strong jaw and down his neck, lingering in the hollow at the base of his throat. Duncan tipped his head back, his low groan vibrating against her lips.

Kimber couldn't resist following the line of his nearest collarbone, her tongue lightly tracing a trail out to his strong shoulder. Loosening her grip on the headboard, she kissed her way over his biceps, paused at his inner elbow, then picked up his hand and brought his fingers to her mouth. After kissing each fingertip she pulled his index finger into the wet heat of her mouth, laving it with her tongue, then added his middle finger and gently sucked on them.

"Oh, hell." He looked down at her. He licked his lips, leaving them wet and inviting. "Are you trying to kill me?"

She glanced up and saw the carnal strain on his face. She released his fingers and murmured, "Let me take care of you."

She let his hand drop back to his side and leaned over him again. She nuzzled his chest, darting her tongue out to flick at one hard nipple. His indrawn breath sounded like the sweetest music to her ears. She rubbed her fingers back and forth over one of his nipples while she licked and sucked the other one.

Deciding she needed both hands, she swung one leg over him and straddled his thighs. His thick erection pressed against the zip of his jeans, and when she let her weight settle over him his breath hissed between his teeth.

Her lips followed the smattering of hair that bisected his tummy. In her eagerness she fumbled a little with the button at the waist of his jeans, but the way his stomach muscles jumped beneath her fingers made her think he didn't mind too much. "Lift your hips," she murmured. His lean hips came up off the bed and she jerked his jeans and underwear down to his knees, baring his cock to her gaze. And her hands.

And her mouth.

But not just yet. Anticipation was the greatest aphrodisiac of all.

Kimber got off the bed and pulled his clothing the rest of the way off, leaving them to fall on the floor. She ran her hands lightly down Duncan's legs, knowing his sexual arousal was increasing his blood flow, heating his body. She loved the feel of warm skin covering hard, flexing muscles. Her pussy thumped with emptiness, her nipples hardened. But this wasn't about her—it was all about him. She kissed a path over one hip to his leg, lingered on the sensitive flesh of his inner thigh, feeling his cock twitch against her cheek.

"Kimber…" His voice rasped against her eardrums, setting up another set of shivers.

With a soft sigh of longing she climbed back onto the bed, settling between his legs. She took his erection in one hand. He was so hot and heavy in her palm, his skin silky smooth. She rubbed the fingers of her other hand lightly over his hair-dusted balls. "What do you want, Duncan? This?" She leaned down and pressed her open mouth against one testicle, letting her warm breath blow against him as she swirled the tip of her tongue in a slow circle. Lifting her head, she whispered, "Or this?" and nibbled her way up the underside of his cock to his tip.

She licked the drop of fluid that wept from the slit. His hips punched upward, driving more of his length into her mouth. She pulled away and *tsked* him. "I'm taking care of you, remember? You're just supposed to lie there and let me do all the work."

"Then get to it." Duncan's irises glowed silver. The wildness of the vampire swallowed up the green and blazed from his eyes. "Stop teasing."

"But the teasing will lead to so much more," Kimber promised and stuck out her tongue to lap at the head of his cock. She held his gaze, exulting in seeing a muscle flex in his taut jaw. He was on the fine edge of his control—she wanted to see if she could shove him over it. Making him shed his cool, controlled exterior was her new calling in life.

For however long that might be.

For however long he might be hers.

She was under no illusions here. He was an immortal; she was not. He wouldn't age past how he appeared now. She would grow old and die, and she somehow didn't think he'd still be with her when her hair was gray and her boobs hung to her waist. And that was being optimistic on her part. She had no guarantee she'd live past today.

And, realistically, with the mood Maddalene was in, neither did he. So *carpe diem* and *carpe penis*.

She looked down at his erection. He was thick and long, wide veins running the length of his shaft. More clear liquid hovered at the tip, and she leaned forward, swiping it with her tongue.

His hands came up and fisted in her hair. "More," he demanded, his voice guttural.

Kimber took the head of his cock into her mouth and sucked lightly. She stroked one hand down his shaft and cupped his balls, rocking them in her fingers.

Duncan groaned and bucked against her. "God. Take more!"

She opened her mouth wide and took as much of him as she could. He was so thick she couldn't take all of him, so she stroked her hand from her mouth down to his base. When he grunted and thrust against her, she drew slowly away until he left her mouth with a soft, wet *pop*.

"Kimber…"

"Anticipation, remember?" She pressed his cock up against his belly and licked a path on the underside from the crown to the base. He tipped his hips toward her, and she smiled in feminine triumph. There was something very empowering about having a strong man like this silently—and sometimes not so silently—begging for more.

She was only too happy to oblige. In her own way.

In her own time.

She swiped the flat of her tongue over his sac and pulled one of his balls into her mouth. Beginning a slow steady stroke of one hand along his shaft, she fingered his balls with the other hand, rolling them back and forth as she nibbled and sucked. She slipped her fingers from his testicles to the sensitive skin behind, rubbing gently.

She licked her way back up the length of his cock then pulled him into her mouth. Keeping one hand beneath him, she palmed his sac and rubbed the skin behind it. He pumped his hips, thrusting more of his cock into her mouth, and she hummed, knowing the vibration would shoot straight through him.

"Damn!" Duncan's hips bucked and surged, driving more of his thick length into her mouth. The head of his cock hit the back of her throat, triggering her gag reflex. She pulled back slightly to catch her breath then went back down.

He tried to push her away, but she swatted at his hands and stayed where she was. She put her hands on his thighs and kept sucking. She loved being able to do this for him, to give him such primal pleasure.

"I'm going to come, sweetheart," he muttered, his muscles tensing beneath her hands. His hands went to her hair and gripped, holding her steady.

Bring it on! Kimber hummed again and brought his cock deeper, to the back of her throat, and swallowed.

He growled and took over the rhythm, driving into her mouth with short, hard thrusts. She opened her mouth as wide as she could and sucked him on each outward stroke. She reached one hand between his legs and grasped his balls, tugging on the hard globes.

His roar reverberated through the small room. Hands tightening in her hair, he held himself still while his release jetted into her mouth. And she loved every last drop.

Hard hands around her arms hoisted her up, and he clamped his mouth over hers in a possessive, demanding kiss. Drawing back, he cupped her face in his hands. "I think you've about killed me." He kissed her again. "Let me return the favor."

With a quick twist of his lean torso, he flipped her over onto her back. He stared for a moment at her lying there, clad only in her bra and panties. His eyes narrowed, and he placed one palm on the slight rise of her tummy. Heat from his big hand permeated her skin, fired her blood. Even with need riding him so high, he still found the strength to handle her gently.

He drew in a deep breath through his nose and groaned. "God, you smell so good when you're aroused." He reached behind her and undid her bra, pulling the filmy material away and letting it drop to the floor. Then he pulled her panties off and let them drop, too.

His hands slid from her ankles up to her knees, parting her legs. He bent over her and pressed his lips to one calf, mouthing a path up her leg to the back of her knee. He draped her leg over his brawny shoulder and lifted her other leg. After placing a soft kiss on her inner thigh he let that leg rest over his shoulder as well. She tensed, wanting him so badly, wanting, needing to feel his mouth against her. Her fingers curled into her palms.

"So pretty here," he murmured, his breath puffing against her mound.

Heat spread in her belly and moved lower, plumping her sex, slicking her core.

He spread her slick folds apart with his thumbs. With another rough growl, he dipped his head and swiped the flat of his tongue along the length of her slit.

Kimber moaned and jerked, tilting her hips and letting her thighs fall apart even more. Duncan's hands slid under her and lifted her closer to his mouth. His low groan vibrated against her clit just before he sucked it into the wet warmth of his mouth.

She helplessly thrust her hips against his face, seeking out more of his touch. As he suckled her swollen bud, his fingers kneaded her buttocks. He brushed against the puckered rosebud of her ass, and she shuddered as her climax began to build.

He licked through her folds to her slick opening. His tongue swirled around and around, making her cry out. She gripped his hair, holding his head close to her, crying out again as he fucked his tongue into her sheath.

He moved back to her clit. One last suckle, and she fell over the edge with a scream. He brought one hand between her legs and slid two long fingers into her pussy, thrusting in and out while she moaned and quaked around him.

When she was finally still, Duncan wiped his hand across his mouth. He let her legs fall from his shoulders and she was content to flop onto the bed like a landed fish. He came up over her and kissed her, giving her a taste of herself.

Kimber tried to calm her breathing. He settled at her side, moving one thick thigh over hers, cupping her breast with his hand. His thumb swept languidly over her tight nipple.

She sighed and rested her hand on his forearm, feeling the muscles flex with the movement of his thumb. She closed her eyes, feeling sated and content for the first time in a long time. "Well, Mr. MacDonnough, I think you've about killed *me*."

His low chuckle stirred the hair at her temple. "Just returning the favor, sweetheart."

All she wanted to do was lie here in his arms and not face reality. But she couldn't. She stirred. "We should go to Natalie and Aodhán."

Duncan's arms tightened around her. "In a minute. I want to hold you a while longer."

Kimber settled down against him again and rubbed her cheek against his hair-roughened chest. It felt good to be in a man's embrace again.

In *this* man's embrace.

He was good and honorable, and in trouble because of her. "Tell me what happened with Maddalene," she murmured. She couldn't keep from touching him, though, rubbing her fingers lightly over the pectoral muscle opposite the one her cheek rested on.

"She wanted you here. She was disappointed when I came without you. When I told her to back off, she called me disloyal and punished me."

At the complete lack of emotion in his voice, she propped up on one elbow and looked down into his face with a frown. "And you...what? Just stood there and let her whip you?"

He shifted a little beneath her but his frank gaze stayed on hers. "If I had fought her, it would have kept her focus on you. I let her vent some of her frustration."

"By turning your back into spaghetti?" She scowled. "Don't do that again."

"I'm almost completely healed, thanks to you."

"Thanks to me you were hurt in the first place." She started to put her head back on his chest but he brought one hand up to her face.

"Don't you even think to take the blame for this, Kimber." His fingers beneath her chin were strong yet gentle. "Maddalene's been working up to something like this for the past several months."

"Why?" she asked. "I don't understand any of it. What's so important to her that she insists on my help? Who is this centuries' old corpse she wants me to reanimate?"

"Her consort, Eduardo."

"Consort?" She felt her eyes go wide as realization struck. "You mean he's a *vampire*?" At his nod, she shook her head. "No. No way. Hell, no."

The edges of his mouth quirked. "Kimber, you need to tell me how you really feel."

"Smartass." She smacked his chest. "She's insane. With a human it would be difficult, but with a vampire? I don't even want to think of the kind of energy it would take to reanimate something that wasn't alive to begin with. I mean, actually, it would be re-reanimating, you know?"

"But could it be done?"

She stared at him. He surely couldn't be suggesting… "No. Duncan, it's too dangerous."

"But could it be done?" he asked again.

"Why? Do you *want* me to do it?"

"No, of course not." He stroked his hand down her cheek. "But unless we can convince Maddalene that there's absolutely no way it can be done, she'll keep pushing."

Kimber bit her lip.

"Can it be done?"

The man was like a demented terrier. She huffed a sigh. "Possibly." When he stared at her, she grimaced. "Look, I've been saying it can't be done because it probably can't. At the very least it shouldn't. Especially now. With what happened to Whitcomb..."

She just wasn't sure anymore. Generally speaking, vampires didn't have souls, so the Unseen didn't really latch onto anything within the body. It just filled it and became something...else. Something different. Dark. If she were more religious she would have called it unholy.

She shook her head. "I just can't guarantee what we'd end up with. There's something unbalanced in the Unseen, Duncan. I felt it with Whitcomb, and I felt it again when I was trying to save Bishop." Tears sprang to her eyes at the thought of her friend, and she blinked them back. At some point she hoped she'd get to mourn Carson Bishop the way he deserved to be mourned, but now was not that time. "If I could somehow manage to reanimate Eduardo, it wouldn't truly be him. It would be something I can't control. Something darker. That much I do know."

"Something darker than a vampire?" He lifted a brow, his expression reminding her of her bias against him and his kind.

She sighed again. "It's the whole biting thing, Duncan. Well, biting and draining."

"I've bitten you twice now, once in passion and once when I was injured, and I didn't lose control. You can trust me, Kimber."

And there was the heart of the matter. She'd been telling herself for months that she couldn't trust Duncan, not with the stuff that counted. Oh, she trusted him to help her fight zombies, but she hadn't trusted him with more than her physical safety. He was part of Maddalene's cadre, and *she* couldn't be trusted.

He was a vampire, the kind of creature that killed her parents. But he was also a man.

Her man.

It was time for her to face her fears and beat those bitches down.

Chapter Eleven

After a shower that was much longer than it needed to be because they couldn't keep their hands off each other, Kimber and Duncan went back to bed and fell asleep in each other's arms. She knew that he needed rest in order for his back to continue healing. She needed it because he'd bitten her again and while he hadn't taken much, it had been enough to make her tired.

A while later movement in the bed woke her. She turned to her side to see him sitting up, rubbing one hand across his face. His dark hair was rumpled, giving him a hot bed head look. "Are you all right?" she asked, pulling herself up to rest against the headboard. "How's your back?"

"I'm good. It's fine," he responded, sliding a hand around the back of her neck and tugging her close for a long, slow kiss. When he drew away, her breath rasped between her lips and her libido had flared to life again.

Damn. The man sure did know how to kiss.

"We need to talk to Aodhán," he said.

She blinked. "Okay, I so wasn't expecting that." She leaned back to look at his face. "And I'm really doing my best not to start freaking out, but when we're in bed together, naked and kissing, and then you go and say we need to talk to Aodhán, all sorts of kinky things start running through my head. He's like my brother, so none of these thoughts end good for you."

His lips twitched. One of these days she'd say something smartass and she'd get a full-blown smile from her dour vampire. It was her new goal in life.

"They're here, too, by the way," she added, realizing he probably didn't know her friends had come along. He might have assumed they would have, because they wouldn't have let Kimber go on her own. "They're out in the living room." She raised her eyebrows. "So, what exactly do we need to talk to Aodhán about?"

"It's something Maddalene said, right before she took the cat to me." He met her gaze. "She told me to ask Aodhán how she feels about males betraying her."

She frowned. "What the hell would he know about it?"

"That's what we need to find out." He rolled out of bed and stretched. His back was completely healed, and only two long, thin scars criss-crossed his lower back. She hoped in time and with a few more feedings even those would fade away.

Her gaze drifted down. God, he had the best, most squeezable ass. It was a work of art, really. She reached over, intending to curl her fingers in those muscled buttocks, but he moved away before she could get him. She gave a little growl of disappointment.

"Get up and put your clothes on, sweetheart." He walked over to a tall bureau and yanked open a drawer. Seconds later he'd tugged a soft-looking pair of gray sweat pants over his lean hips. A chest-hugging black T-shirt followed. "We need to get this sorted out and make sure Aodhán really is on our side."

Kimber frowned. "How can you even ask that?" She got out of bed and pulled on her clothing. The floor was cold against her feet. "Can I have a pair of socks?" she asked, and added, "Aodhán doesn't have to prove anything."

"No?" His deep voice held a hardness she'd heard before, and it usually pissed her off because he was being stubborn and autocratic with her. She didn't want him turning that attitude on Aodhán. He yanked open another drawer and tossed her a pair of white athletic socks.

She sat on the bed and pulled them on, then hurried across the room as Duncan opened the bedroom door and headed down the hallway toward the living room.

"No, he doesn't." She trailed him, grabbing onto his T-shirt to try to slow him down. It was like trying to stop an elephant by yanking on its tail. Didn't work worth spit.

The smell of cinnamon and cloves was still present and she saw flames burning brightly in the fireplace. The room was a little on the cool side, but pleasant enough in the area near the fire.

"Who doesn't what?" Aodhán asked from his sprawled position on the sofa.

Natalie was at the dining room table, eating Chinese. She looked up. Before Kimber or Duncan could respond to Aodhán's question, Natalie said, "Did you know they have a chef here? So the human groupies who live here can be well-fed." She looked at Duncan. "If you'd told me Maddalene had a five-star chef here,

I would've been here six months ago. God, this is so good." She forked another bite into her mouth.

Kimber felt Duncan tense up. "Who brought that?" he asked.

She wasn't too thrilled, either. At least one more person possibly knew that there were humans in Duncan's rooms.

Natalie gave a nonchalant wave. "That cutie patootie Atticus," she said around the food in her mouth. "He said not to worry, that he told the chef it was for Maddalene's attendants. Nobody ever questions a request from the queen, apparently." Her eyes widened. "Man, that Atticus is something else. Talk about gorgeous." She fanned herself with her hand. "He's an eyegasm for sure."

Aodhán grunted. "He's also a bloodsucker. He's probably just trying to fatten you up, did you ever think about that?" When she gave him a one-fingered salute, he turned his attention back to Duncan. "Who doesn't what?" he asked again.

"You don't have to explain yourself," Kimber responded, more for Duncan than for Aodhán. She scurried around her back-to-being-a-pain-in-the-ass vampire and went to stand next to Aodhán.

The fey warrior scowled and rose to his feet. "Explain myself about what?"

Duncan folded his arms across his chest, his entire stance aggressive. "Maddalene told me I should ask you how she feels about men betraying her. What do you have to say about that?"

"Duncan, don't be such a—" Kimber began.

"Look at his face," he interrupted.

She glanced at Aodhán. Color rode high on his cheekbones and he wouldn't meet Duncan's eyes. "Aodhán?" she asked, turning to fully face him. "Are you…" She swallowed. "God, are you involved with Maddalene?"

His fierce gaze shot to her. "Hell, no." He drew in a deep breath and blew it out on a sigh. "Not anymore."

"When exactly were you involved with Maddalene?" Duncan's terse voice radiated anger. "And why am I just hearing about it?"

"It was a long time ago, before you ever met her. Before Eduardo even."

"But she and Eduardo were together for almost three hundred years." Duncan let out a low whistle.

Aodhán dipped his head just a little, as if he was ashamed. "It was five hundred years ago, give or take a few years."

Duncan raised an arrogant brow. "It must have been something if she's still mad about it."

"Are you kidding?" Aodhán's lips thinned. "She holds onto grudges better than a sponge holds water."

"Maybe somebody should just squeeze her," Kimber muttered. "I know I'd like to pop her head like a pimple." She wondered for a fleeting moment if Duncan had ever been Maddalene's boy toy then pushed the thought away. It didn't matter. She knew he wasn't now. He wouldn't take her to bed if he was shtupping the queen. He was more honorable than that.

Aodhán gave a snort of laughter. "I appreciate the sentiment but not the visual. Thanks for that." He finally looked at Duncan. "It was a bright flame that burned out quickly. It didn't set well with her that I was the one to end it."

"What happened?" Kimber asked. "You finally realized what a queen-sized bitch she is?"

Aodhán's eyes went flinty. "She attacked one of my people and nearly killed her." When everyone looked at him without saying anything, he gave a low growl. "I'd been letting her bite me, but she wanted more. She wanted to gorge herself on fey blood. I refused to let her and ended the relationship." He shook his head. "She had the balls to question why I called things off with her."

"This doesn't make sense." Kimber glanced between the two men. "Why would she see you protecting one of your people as being disloyal? If anything, she was the disloyal one for attacking someone you cared about."

"Exactly."

Duncan went still as only a vampire can. She looked at him, unable to read from his expression what was going on behind it. "Duncan?"

His gaze shot to her face. "I've been a fucking idiot."

"Okay." She took a few steps toward him. "Just so we're all on the same page, what do you think you've been an idiot about?"

His lips did that twitching thing he did when he was trying not to smile. Damn it. She'd almost gotten him.

"You say that like there's more than one thing."

"You say that like there's not."

And finally, she got what she was after. His lips twitched again and then a wide grin lit his entire face. He was a good-looking man when he wore his usual somber expression, but when he smiled…

He was irresistible.

She went over and wrapped her arms around his waist, giving him a bear hug. His arms went around her back and he chuckled, the sound reverberating against her ear where it was pressed to his chest. She loosened her hold and went up on her tiptoes to press a kiss to one corner of his mouth. "You should do that more often," she whispered.

"Do what?"

"Laugh. You're a gorgeous thing when you laugh."

Now he was the one with pink zinging his cheeks.

She gaped. Duncan MacDonnough, mean, lean, vampire machine, was blushing?

"Brat," he muttered and swatted her rear with one broad palm. The smack was hard enough to sting, but the slight pain turned into simmering pleasure within seconds.

"Tease," she murmured with a wink. She turned and went back to the sofa, plopping down and pulling up her feet to sit cross-legged. "So, what exactly do you think is idiotic?"

He made a face. "That my loyalties have been misplaced." At her questioning look, he said, "I've been supporting Maddalene blindly for years out of a sense of duty. In return she has been threatening you off and on for six months and had me beaten."

"So, what do we do now?" she asked.

Both men sat down, and Natalie wandered in from the kitchen. She sat on the couch next to Kimber and let out a little burp. "Sorry," she said with a grin. She patted her stomach. "Man, I haven't eaten like that in months."

"You've probably had too much and will get sick." Aodhán turned a frowning face her way.

Kimber saw the concern in his gaze, but apparently all Natalie saw was censure because she flipped him the bird. "If I do, I'll be sure to puke all over you and your mighty sword."

"Nat," Kimber murmured.

The other woman huffed a sigh and shoved back into the corner of the sofa. "Don't mind me," she said with a wave. "Carry on while I sit here and let all that yummy food digest."

Duncan leaned forward in his chair. "Kimber, can the Unseen be used to do something other than reanimate the dead?"

"Why do you ask?" She had no idea where this was coming from. "If you're asking me to reconsider Maddalene's request—"

"No!" His eyes flared. "I believe you when you say it will take too much from you. I don't want to endanger you." He paused and dropped his gaze to his hands. "I just wondered if you could tap into the Unseen for other purposes."

"I suppose so. I mean, I'd like to figure out what in the Unseen started all of this, but I don't know what other purposes you're talking about."

"Say, hypothetically, someone wanted to…reinvigorate themselves." He looked up at her. "Could you do that with the Unseen?"

Her brows drew down. "Reinvigorate? What, like use the Unseen as some sort of supernatural Viagra?"

"Oh, hell." Aodhán slouched down in his chair. "I don't want to be in this conversation if that's where things are headed."

"I do." Natalie perked up, sitting straighter.

Duncan huffed an aggrieved sigh. For someone who didn't need to breathe, he spent an awful lot of time sighing. Probably just around her, though, to be fair. All those sighs would be worth it if she could wring another laugh out of him.

"Not supernatural Viagra," he muttered. He raked his hand through his hair, the dark strands staying tousled, giving him an even hotter bed head look than he'd had before.

"Then what?" When he seemed reluctant to explain, Kimber

got up and went over to him. He sat back in surprise and she plopped onto his lap. "Talk to me, Duncan. What exactly are you asking?"

He slid an arm around her waist, supporting her, and the other arm rested across her thighs. Her nearness affected him; she felt the press of his erection against her hip and tried to stay still. As much as she might like to jump that particular bone, they had an audience and she wasn't an exhibitionist. Plus she had a feeling this was important to him. If it was, she wanted to help if she could.

Wow. How far she'd come in only a few days. It was too bad she couldn't stay here in this room, just her and Duncan, and forget about zombies and other vampires. But that wasn't possible. Not now.

"Tell me," she said softly.

He seemed to take some measure of strength from her nearness. The hand resting on the outer curve of her thigh tightened. "I haven't felt alive in so long, Kimber," he murmured. His husky voice wrapped around her, tugging on everything feminine within her. "I wanted…I need to feel emotions again." He grimaced. "I mean, stronger than I do. Like I used to when I was human. I thought maybe if I could touch the Unseen, if you'd be my conduit, I could grab something. Anything to make me feel again."

* * *

Duncan felt her refusal before she shook her head. She seemed to withdraw into herself.

"I can't, Duncan." She climbed off his lap and walked over to the fireplace to stare into the flames. "The only way I've called upon the Unseen is when I'm touching a dead body. It reanimates briefly and then I send the Unseen back to itself. I've never tried it with someone who was walking and talking. I'm not even sure how that would work." She shook her head. "I've wondered if my ability is why most vampires seem uncomfortable around me, like they're afraid I could somehow de-animate them, but I've never tried it. I certainly haven't ever tried to do what you're asking, so just don't. Don't ask me to do this."

He rose to his feet and went to stand behind her. He didn't touch her, but he knew she realized he was behind her because her back went stiff. "The hope of touching the Unseen has been the only thing keeping me going these last few years, Kimber. I need to try." Tamping down the natural arrogance that vampirism wrought, he added a quiet, "Please."

"I can't."

"Can't or won't?" He fought back his rising anger. "The last six months I've protected you, provided for you, and you can't be bothered to do this one thing for me?" He hadn't asked anything else of her. Well, other than asking her to trust him not to drain her, to give him a chance with her lovely body. But this. This was important to him, too.

She turned to face him. Indecision flickered across her face, darkened her eyes. "You remember Whitcomb?" she finally muttered. "The Unseen has…changed."

"Tell him, Kimber," Aodhán said. "Or I will."

She glared at the fey warrior, her small hands fisting at her sides. "Fine. I will." Her shoulders slumped. "I was going to anyway, Aodhán. You don't need to tattle on me." She glanced at him and then at Natalie. "But I'd like some privacy."

Without looking away from Kimber, Duncan motioned toward the hallway. "I converted one of the bedrooms to a home theater. When we lost power I turned it into my library. Plenty of books in there, and once you close the door it's pretty much soundproof."

"All right. Come on, Nat." Aodhán started down the hallway.

"But…" Natalie didn't budge from her vantage point on the sofa.

"Natalie." Aodhán's voice was deep and rumbly. He sounded very much in charge and like he wasn't going to put up with any more of Natalie's bull. Duncan didn't doubt for a second that if she didn't get her ass moving Aodhán would haul her over his shoulder and carry her out.

"Oh, fine." Natalie huffed and got off the couch, grumbling under her breath the whole way to Aodhán.

Duncan waited until he heard the door to the library close behind them, then he faced Kimber. When she didn't say anything, he raised one eyebrow and folded his arms over his chest.

"Oh, don't pull that silence thing on me," she muttered. She ran her fingers through her hair. "When you were being used as Maddalene's whipping boy—that bitch!—I talked Aodhán into helping me catch a zombie."

"What!" Duncan surged forward and grasped her shoulders. "What were you thinking?"

She shrugged away from him. "I was thinking that if I could figure out how to drive the Unseen out of one zombie, I might be able to figure out how to do it on a wider scale."

Damn it, the woman would try a saint, and he wasn't even close to being one. "What happened?"

"We chained it up to one of the vending machines in the basement. I stayed out of its reach," she rushed to add. "I got on the floor and touched its ankle. Which, by the way, gross! Dead people skin is one thing, but rotting dead people skin is…just ew."

"Kimber," he grated in warning. "Stay on topic."

She frowned. "Me touching zombie skin is very much on topic, Duncan."

"Kimber." Why he felt the need for a bracing gulp of whiskey was beyond him. But what did it say about her that she could drive a vampire to drink, and not in a good way?

"When I reached for the Unseen in him, this raw energy surged up." Her eyes were huge as she looked at him. "Just like that night with Richard Whitcomb. It lunged for me, and it was wrong." She spread her hands. "It used to be light, swirling energy in hues of the rainbow. But now it's tainted, like it's covered by a huge, oily mantle of evil."

He ground his jaw. He was going to kill Aodhán for taking part in something this foolhardy. The fey warrior should have known better. "And?" he asked.

"The zombie went crazy. He almost got loose. Whatever it was that was animating him, whatever dark, wicked part of the Unseen was inside of him, was strengthened by my contact with it and the greater part of the Unseen." She wrapped her arms around her waist. "Don't you see, Duncan? It's too dangerous for me to tap into the Unseen now. It could…" She shook her head.

His anger faded and was overtaken by concern. He went to her and drew her into his arms. "What are you afraid it will do?"

"I'm afraid it will overtake *me*. Turn *me* into something evil." She bit her lip.

"I won't let that happen, sweetheart."

"How would you stop it? Even if you'd been with me and Aodhán, how would you have stopped it from taking over me if I hadn't broken away in time?"

And just that fast his anger was back. "You were an idiot to try something like that without me."

Her eyes widened. Nostrils flared, she gritted, "Don't you dare call me an idiot, you arrogant bastard. You couldn't have done anything Aodhán didn't do. Anyway, I'll do what I think is best when I think it's best."

"No, you won't." Fire raced into his eyes and he knew his irises had gone silver. His fangs dropped over his lower lip. He dropped his hands to his sides and widened his stance. She didn't look the least bit intimidated.

"Listen, you." She straightened her index finger and poked him in the chest. "I'm the one who decided to rush over here and let you bite me so you could be healed. Otherwise you'd still be a mass of hamburger meat lying in there on your bed. So a little gratitude might be in order." She gave him another hard poke. "You are not the boss of me."

"Actually, I am." Duncan swept her into his arms and carried her into his bedroom, ignoring the way she struggled in his arms and sputtered insults and threats. If there was one way to get through to her, it was through sex. He'd orgasm her strident attitude out of her until she was soft and pliant. He slammed the door closed with his heel and strode to the bed.

When he dropped her onto it, she quickly scrambled off to

the other side and watched him warily. "Duncan, whatever you're thinking about doing, don't."

"I'm thinking about sinking my cock inside you. I'm thinking I'll fuck you until you scream my name, and then I'll fuck you some more." He started to move around the bed toward her, watching slight fear and deeper arousal skate across her face. "I'm thinking you'll like it. A lot."

"I don't want this. I don't want you." Her gaze flickered from him to the bed and back again. He could tell she was gauging the distance and trying to decide when she'd need to try to get across the bed before he could reach her. He didn't mind. He was faster than she was.

"Little liar."

She took a step backward. "I'm not lying. I don't want you."

He let his eyes drift over her body and drew in her scent on a deep inhalation. "I can see your nipples. They're hard. You want my mouth on you, sucking your nipples, your clit. You want me to shove my tongue inside you." He gave her a slow smile, a wicked smile that should let her know his intentions. "Don't deny it, sweetheart. I can smell your arousal. I bet your panties are wet, aren't they?"

"That's…leftover from the shower because you can't keep your hands to yourself, you sex fiend." She crossed her arms. "And if my nipples are hard it's because I'm mad." She narrowed her eyes at him. "These are angry nipples, not aroused ones."

Even when she was lying and being sassy, she drew him like no other woman ever had. With a click of his tongue he shook his head. "Those are aching nipples," he said in a voice gone husky. "And I have plans for them."

Chapter Twelve

Kimber stared at Duncan. Her heart went from pounding in her chest to pounding in her sex. She clamped her jaws together. *Don't you dare get any wetter,* she told her weak-willed pussy. But damn! His predatory stalk toward her had done something to her willfulness. Who knew she had a streak of submissive in her?

But she held on to her anger. She wasn't going to make this easy for him. If she let him have her without a fight, that would set the tone for their relationship. She'd meant it when she'd told him he wasn't her boss. She wasn't averse to discussing things with him, but ultimately it was her life, her decision.

She wasn't stupid. She knew she couldn't outrun a vampire. But she'd give him a good chase. Keeping her eyes on him, she lunged forward, leaping onto the bed and over it, surprising even herself with her agility. She heard him growl behind her and he caught her at the door.

"Where do you think you're going?" he whispered in her ear. "I said I have plans."

She twisted in his hold. If he got his hands or his mouth on her nipples, her resistance would die a quick death. She drew up her foot and stomped her bare heel as hard as she could onto his instep. A satisfying low hiss came from behind her, and his hands loosened from around her upper arms. She jerked away from him and headed toward the bathroom.

Before she could reach the door, he stood in front of it. "Stupid vampire speed," she muttered as she back pedaled. Her eyes darted around for an avenue of escape even while she realized there was none.

"Give it up, sweetheart." He stalked forward, loose hipped and big cocked.

She held up a hand, like that would ward him off. "You just keep your distance, Duncan. You're not going to touch me."

His eyes glinted. "That sounds like a challenge to me." Lustful anticipation crossed his face.

Kimber went very still. Even her breath seemed suspended. Oh, hell. Why not? Why was she holding back? Sex with Duncan was great. More than great. But, admittedly, she didn't want him to think she was easy or anything.

"If you think you're man enough," she drawled, flipping her hand around and crooking her index finger at him, "then come and get me."

Another wicked smile curved his mouth. *Good God, be careful what you wish for, girl.* She'd wanted to see him smile more, and this…She felt another rush of moisture slick the lips of her sex.

He yanked his T-shirt off and let it fall to the floor. A tug at his waist and his sweatpants came down. He kicked them off and started forward again. His cock rose out of a nest of dark curls, the tip reaching toward his belly button, he was so hard. Lust rolled off him in waves, making her shiver in anticipation and wonder if maybe this wasn't such a good idea after all. Maybe she'd awakened a beast when she should have left well enough alone.

But what a sexy beast he was.

She backed up until she couldn't go any farther. Palms flat against the wall, she stared at him, her pulse pounding madly in her throat. She felt alive, like she hadn't in years. Only Duncan, a supposedly soulless bloodsucking fiend, had ever made her feel quite like this, like she was standing on a cliff, ready to jump, knowing he'd be there at the bottom to catch her.

He stared at her, his eyes as wild as a storm. Her body picked up on the message in his eyes and heat traveled from her core. Her nipples beaded tighter, her stomach clenched. She bit the inside of her cheek to restrain the moan that wanted to erupt out of her mouth. The powerful grip of this need he aroused in her so easily, so quickly, was insanity.

He stopped in front of her, his big, bare feet braced wide. Muscles worked over his body in rolling curves, veins snaking along massive biceps. His shoulders looked like they went on forever, his broad chest narrowed to a lean waist and hips, and long, strong legs.

But it was the expression on his face, the look in his eyes, that riveted her. So much desperate need, for *her*. Suddenly she didn't want to fight him anymore. She needed him just as much. Now.

Hard.

Fast.

Deep.

* * *

Duncan stared at Kimber. She was spoiling for a fight, and with the fear still riding him at the chance she'd taken with her life, he was primed to give it to her. If she wanted to do this the hard way, he was more than happy to oblige. Desire throbbed deep in his gut and danced along his veins to pulse behind his eyes.

He could smell her arousal, see the way her heart pounded against her ribs, making the skin above quiver with each beat. That same beat pounded in her creamy throat.

It wasn't fear. He'd have sensed that. Smelled it, even. No, she was nervous, even a little apprehensive, but she wasn't afraid. He didn't want her frightened of him, but a healthy dose of respect for his strength and his right to protect her wouldn't be unwelcome.

He took the steps necessary to bring them face to face. Leaning one forearm against the wall beside her head, he bent until his lips were a breath away from hers. "Do you think I'm man enough?" He grabbed her hand and wrapped her fingers around his erection. She gave him a squeeze, and he couldn't stop the moan. "Damn it, sweetheart. That feels so good."

Her tongue swept across her bee-stung lips, leaving them wet and inviting.

"Tell me you don't want this, and mean it," he said, "and it all stops right now." If there was a God in heaven she wouldn't tell him no.

She shook her head, her gaze locked with his. The hazel of her irises was more green than brown now, almost swallowed up by the pupils. "I do want this, Duncan. I do want you."

He pressed his hips against hers, letting her feel his hardness against her soft belly. Her lips parted on a gasp. He took her mouth with his, hard, unable to summon gentleness through the wild arousal beating at him.

Duncan brought his hands up, cupping Kimber's face between his palms, and tilted her head for a better angle. She tasted better than anything he could remember. Sweet like honey with a hint of something tart. She tasted like...

Home.

He cursed softly and gentled his caress. With Kimber he felt, sometimes too much. But he could hardly walk around with her attached to his cock all the time.

He touched her lips softly and laved their seam with his tongue. She opened slowly and captured his tongue, drawing it deeper into her mouth. Her tongue twisted around his, tasting him, devouring him. She was like a raging wildfire, so beautiful in her desire that he wanted to protect her and take her over in a maelstrom all at the same time.

Her scent made him crazy with need, and her touch—soft and hungry and searching—made him ravenous. Her fingers still curled around his cock, alternating between light and hard strokes until he finally had to move her hand off him. He wanted to be inside her when he came.

With eager hands he eased off her clothing. Pink-tipped breasts billowed above her narrow waist and generous hips. He bent his head and kissed her again, sweeping his tongue into her mouth to mate with hers. Her hands came around him, fingers flexing into his back. She moved her legs restlessly. He slid between them, his cock stiff against her belly.

He scattered kisses across her chest and tongued each stiff nipple before kneeling to kiss his way down her flat stomach. He parted her thighs just a little wider and stroked his fingers in a long caress along the slick folds of her sex. She jumped, jerking against his hand, a sharp cry of pleasure escaping her.

He pushed a finger slowly inside her hot, tight sheath. At once her muscles clenched around him, velvet soft yet firm and wet. His own body throbbed and swelled in response. Her hips pressed forward. Duncan thrust another finger into her, stretching her, preparing her. More than anything her pleasure mattered to him. Her velvet folds pulsed for him, wanting, demanding, and he fed that hunger, pushing deep, retreating, thrusting again so that her hips followed his lead.

"That's it, sweetheart," he breathed against her stomach. "Just like that. I want you ready for me."

"I am ready," she panted. Her slender hands grasped his hair, alternately tugging and pushing at him as if she wasn't sure if she wanted his mouth on her clit or higher up.

"No, you're not. Not yet." He flicked his tongue at the swollen nub of flesh at the top of her slit. Her breath hissed out and he tasted her. His name was a whispered plea. He lifted his head to look at her. "Open your legs wider. Let me have you."

To his surprise, she shook her head. "No more playing, Duncan. I want you inside me. Now."

Who was he to argue? He rocketed to his feet, lifting her by her hips and thrusting his cock into her wet heat in one long glide until his balls rested against the curve of her ass. He waited a moment, allowing her body to adjust to his invasion, then he pulled out until only the head of his cock breached her opening. He surged forward again, watching her face for signs of discomfort. She wore only a look of passion, her eyes glazed, her breath coming in pants.

Satisfied she felt the same pleasure he did, he began to move, gliding in and out of her, going deep with each stroke. He tilted her hips so he could hit her clit with each forward movement. Each thrust bumped her against the wall and she moaned and gasped, her hands clutching his shoulders for support.

His own climax roiled through him, drawing his balls up against his body, swelling his cock even more. He buried himself to the hilt, shoving deep, and felt the spasms of her orgasm overtake her. She cried out, throwing her head back, baring her throat to him.

With an animalistic snarl he took what she offered, biting into her soft flesh as he pounded into her, the explosion of his climax ripping through him from his balls to the top of his head.

When he could make his mind work again, he eased fangs and cock out of her. Her inner muscles clung to his sated shaft, making him groan at the renewing pleasure. Sweeping her into his arms, he carried her into the bathroom and gently cleaned her, then took her back into the bedroom and laid her on his bed. He came down next to her and tucked her against his side, content for the first time in a very long time. The sex between them might have started out angry, but it had ended in love.

He stilled then closed his eyes. He couldn't deny it to himself any longer. He loved Kimber. But could he admit it to her? What kind of power over him would his feelings give her?

Her heavy sigh drew his focus outward. "What is it, sweetheart?" he asked, running one palm gently up and down her forearm where it lay across his abdomen.

"I wish we could stay like this," she whispered. "No other vampires. No zombies. Just you and me."

"Me, too." But they couldn't stay like this. Sooner rather than later Maddalene would find Kimber here. Duncan was prepared to fight to the death to protect his love. And he had to win, because otherwise he would leave Kimber unprotected. He couldn't expect Atticus or even Aodhán to care for her like he did.

* * *

The next few days passed in a pleasant blur for Kimber. She and Duncan settled into their relationship, spending the nights pleasuring each other and the days talking and getting to know each other better. Natalie and Aodhán helped to pass the time, and even seemed to be getting along better as well. They all knew they had to decide what they were going to do once Maddalene returned, because they were also certain their time was running out.

On this particular morning Duncan had gone to talk with Atticus about additional security for them. He wanted his friend's advice on which vampires they could trust to remain loyal to the two of them instead of their queen. Natalie and Aodhán sat at the dining room table, working a crossword puzzle together, while Kimber sprawled on the sofa reading a cozy mystery.

She heard a commotion at the door and looked up to see it swing open and Maddalene breeze in. The guards Atticus had posted were crumpled on the floor. Kimber jumped to her feet, holding the book in both hands in front of her, like it would somehow protect her.

She saw Aodhán motion for Natalie to remain where she was then he walked over and stood next to Kimber. "Maddalene," he said, his voice deep and dark. "What do you want?"

Her dark gaze swept over them. "I was gone nearly a week and return to find I have visitors I knew nothing about. I want to talk with Kimber. Alone."

"Not going to happen." He put one hand on the hilt of his sword.

"Fine. What I have to say isn't private." She glided forward and sank gracefully onto the end of the sofa. Her eyes fastened on Kimber. "I want you to raise my Eduardo. I will give you whatever you ask."

Kimber felt like her heart would jump out of her chest, it was beating so hard. From Maddalene's slight smirk she had a feeling the vampire queen could hear the mad thumping beat. But still she forced herself to meet the other woman's eyes and say with calm assurance, "There's nothing you can offer that would get me to do it. It's too dangerous."

"Really? Nothing at all will sway you?" She stood and walked closer, ignoring Aodhán's protective stance. She tilted her head to one side and studied Kimber in silence for a few seconds. Finally she said, "I smell Duncan on you. The two of you have been intimate." Silver bled into her irises and a hint of fangs appeared over her plump lips. "Perhaps I do have something you'd be interested in after all."

Kimber knew she'd hate herself for asking, but she did anyway. "What's that?"

"Your lover's guaranteed safety. And your own and your friend's as well," she said with a gesture toward Natalie.

Upon being noticed, Natalie's face paled and her eyes widened.

Maddalene glared at Aodhán. "You, however, have no guarantees. The longer you stay, the closer death comes to you."

"If I can take you with me, it would be worth it." Hatred and rage seethed in his voice.

Maddalene lifted one slender shoulder. "That's a big if," she stated in a cold, quiet voice.

He drew his sword. "I could take your head right now."

Before he could say another word, Maddalene moved with preternatural speed to stand behind Natalie, one slim hand wrapped around Natalie's throat. "You try it, my love, and this one will die, too. Are you prepared to make that sacrifice?"

Kimber's heart stuttered in fear even as rage built. She had to diffuse this situation or Natalie would die. Kimber put out a hand. "Aodhán, please."

"Listen to Kimberly, Aodhán. Is sacrificing this innocent human worth taking your vengeance against me?"

He let loose a soft growl but sheathed his sword. Maddalene moved to the door and opened it. "Think about my offer, Kimberly," she said. With a glance at Natalie, she added, "And think about all you have to lose if you refuse." She turned to leave. "Why, Duncan," she all but purred. "I was just welcoming your guests." The hard look she shot him, at odds with the sultry tone of her voice, left very little doubt in Kimber's mind that Duncan was still on Maddalene's shit list.

"I bet you were." His tone was hard, as was the look he shot in the room.

Two vampires with him bent over their fallen comrades in the corridor. Kimber saw one shake his head, and from the somber looks on their faces she realized Maddalene had killed the two who had been guarding the room. The newcomers took up protective stances, their backs to the wall opposite Duncan's front door.

When Duncan saw that Kimber and the others were safe, his shoulders relaxed. "What do you want?" he asked, putting his attention back on Maddalene.

"Nothing that I haven't wanted all along." As she walked by him she trailed a finger along his biceps. "You have a decision to make." With that sultry comment, she turned down the hallway and disappeared from sight.

Duncan strode into the room and slammed the door behind him. He came up to Kimber and pulled her into his arms. "Are you all right?" he asked, his face buried in the curve of her neck.

"Fine. A little shaken. She always makes me as nervous as a cat in a dog kennel." She wrapped her arms around his back and closed her eyes, letting herself feel secure in his embrace. "She threatened us."

He drew back to look into her face. "Who's us?" he asked.

"All of us," Natalie said in a subdued voice as she walked into the living room. Aodhán went to her and put an arm around her waist, hugging her to his side. That she allowed it told Kimber how upset her friend was. Or maybe those two really had decided to bury the hatchet, and not in each other's backs as she might have thought.

Kimber stared into Duncan's eyes. "She told me she would guarantee my safety and Natalie's. And yours."

He rocked back on his heels. "She threatened *me?*"

"She knows we were intimate." She closed her eyes briefly, try-ing to push back the lingering fear. "We're not safe here, Duncan. None of us." She reached up and cupped his jaw in one hand. "We all have to leave. You, me, Nat and Aodhán. Otherwise…"

He nodded. Grim-faced he pressed a gentle kiss on her mouth and then went back to the front door. He opened it and told one of the new guards, "Fetch Atticus."

Kimber saw that the bodies of the two slain vampires had been removed. She hadn't known them, but anyone who got on Mad-dalene's bad side trying to protect Duncan was all right in her book. She was sorry they had died, even if they were vamps.

In just a few minutes his gladiator friend was there. As the two vampires talked, Natalie gave a sigh, her gaze fixed on Dun-can's handsome friend. Aodhán scowled and jerked her closer. She glanced at him with a frown, clearly—to Kimber, any-way—asking him without words what his problem was. "I can't help it that he's so gorgeous," she whispered. "You can't blame a girl for looking."

"Yes, I can." Aodhán's scowl deepened.

Kimber saw Atticus shoot a glance at Natalie. When she real-ized he was looking at her, she blushed. He dropped one eyelid in a flirtatious wink and her cheeks fired even more.

After a few more minutes he and Duncan finished their low-voiced conversation, and Atticus left. Duncan closed the door and went into his bedroom. Kimber followed him in and watched while he gathered some clothing and a few personal items and stuffed them in a large duffle bag.

He zipped it closed. Staring down at it, his hands holding the straps, he murmured. "I'm sorry."

"For what?"

He looked at her then, and tears came to her eyes at the self-loathing she saw in his eyes. "For being arrogant and telling you over and over that you'd be safe here. How can I keep you safe from Maddalene when I can't even protect myself?"

"Duncan…"

He shook his head. "Don't, Kimber. There's nothing you can say to make this situation any better. While the enclave would have protected us against zombies, it would also keep us prisoners here and subject to Maddalene's whims. We need to get out of here."

Then he grabbed her hand and tugged her out of the bedroom. They collected Natalie and Aodhán and some flashlights in addition to the weapons they still carried with them, and the four of them left Duncan's rooms. She expected resistance against them leaving the compound, but the way was clear.

"It's too easy," Natalie said, her words an eerie déjà vu of their arrival days before. But when they passed through the outer gates without trouble, Kimber relaxed a little. They still had to get to the apartment complex safely, but if their luck held, hopefully there wouldn't be too many zombies between them and their destination.

Half an hour later her hopes were not just dashed, they were obliterated. She stood, her back to Duncan's, Aodhán by her side with Natalie's back to his, the four of them surrounded by a horde.

And behind the horde stood a ring of vampires.

The queen bitch had set them up.

Chapter Thirteen

I told you it was too easy," Natalie muttered.

Kimber met her friend's gaze. As much as she tried to stay positive, this could be it. They might die here at the hands and teeth of these things she'd unknowingly created.

"We're gonna die." Natalie's voice was quiet. Fatalistic. "Even if we can fight our way through the zombies, we'll be too tired to take on a bunch of vampires."

"Never say quit," Aodhán said. He held his sword straight out, pointing at the zombies in front of him, his stance preparing him to slice and hack at the enemy. "While we have breath, we have hope."

"Right then." Kimber drew a deep breath and looked at Duncan. "How about you take the thirty on the left and I'll take the twenty on the right?"

His jaw was tight, his eyes brilliant silver. "I've failed you again. I'm sorry."

"Don't be an idiot," she said, putting her gaze back on the

zombies who were shuffling ever closer. In another thirty seconds they'd be close enough to fight. "This isn't your fault."

No one was to blame except her. And she needed to fix it. She focused her energy inward then shot it out toward the Unseen. She'd never tried this without touching a dead person, but she had to do something. As she pushed harder, sweat broke out on her brow, trickled down the side of her face. Without anchoring herself to another human, to the spark of soul remaining in the body, she couldn't quite latch on to anything. Then, like a strike of flint to stone, she felt it.

A swell of responding power rippled toward her. Then there was no time to think, no time to feel, only time to act. As she swung her hatchet at zombie after zombie, she was aware of the others doing the same and, in the background, always in the background, were the vampires, waiting to see if they were needed to finish what the zombies had started.

And still she reached for that supernatural energy, trying to bend it to her will. Her vision went black around the edges, and she fought to hang on to consciousness. When a zombie got too close and she had to wrap her hands around its wrists to hold it off while she tried to catch her breath, she used the connection to delve further into the Unseen. Then, like it had before, that malevolent power surged toward her, and this time, instead of fighting it, she let it wrap its dark claws into her psyche.

Getting one foot up onto the zombie's belly, she shoved it back and sliced her hatchet into the forehead of another. Bodies piled up around them, and still they came. And the vampires watched.

She could hear the grunts from Aodhán and Natalie behind

her, and a quick glance to her side showed that Duncan remained in excellent fighting condition. But they couldn't last. Even a vampire and a fey warrior would eventually tire. Being immortal didn't mean you couldn't be killed. It just took extra effort. And she'd say a zombie horde followed by mean-ass vampires would qualify as extra effort.

As the power of the Unseen intensified, her gut cramped and her knees buckled. She went hot then cold. Only by sheer force of will and a driving desire to stay alive did she manage to keep on her feet. As more and more of the Unseen flowed into her, sweat broke out all over her body and her muscles began to tremble. With a snarl she drew upon the malignant power surging from the Unseen and threw it out at the zombies. Floating spots of light sparkled across her field of vision, those dancing lights that meant her blood pressure was dangerously high. She kept pushing the power outward.

Her heartbeat thundered in her ears. Pain stabbed in her head. Still she pushed. Her heart stuttered then doggedly beat on. From a distance she heard Duncan call out her name, knew he could see the condition she was in. And still she pushed.

Nothing happened. Failure was like bitter ash in her mouth. She stopped focusing on the Unseen, letting it go even though her body held a light buzz; her skin was tingling all over. She had to turn her attention full-time to keeping the zombies from biting her.

Duncan kicked a zombie away from her while shoving his tire iron through the skull of another. Kimber swung her hatchet again and again, the muscles in her shoulders and arms burning with fatigue. Then she noticed a stutter in the shuffling movements. Without being physically touched, one by one the zombies began to drop to the ground.

Soon those zombies within fighting distance were down, unmoving.

She let her hand fall to her side, holding her hatchet in a loose grip. God, her entire body ached now, and her head felt like it was going to explode. She winced with pain and turned toward Duncan. Without thinking she went into his open arms and leaned into his strength.

"What the…" Natalie's stunned, breathless voice brought Kimber's attention to her.

"Are you all right?" Kimber asked, noting her own breathless state.

Natalie nodded.

"Aodhán?" From within the circle of Duncan's arms, Kimber checked on the fey warrior.

"Good here, too." He wasn't as out of breath as she and Natalie were, but for once he'd had to exert himself in battle. He actually sounded invigorated.

Natalie gestured at the bodies lying around them. "Did you do this?" she asked.

"I think so." Dizziness assailed her and her legs gave way. Duncan tightened his hold and supported her. She looked at the vampires hovering all around them. She didn't have anything left in her to fight them off, but hopefully they couldn't tell from where they were. "I just did something I shouldn't have been able to," she called out. "I tapped into the Unseen without touching anyone, and I used it to stop the zombies. Shall I see if I can do the same thing to vampires as I just did to zombies?"

Duncan's fingers tightened around her waist. She leaned into him, trying to tell him without words that she was bluffing. Not only would she not endanger him while trying to wipe out his fellow bloodsuckers, she also didn't think she had anything left to throw at a cute, fluffy little puppy, let alone a dozen or so vamps.

One second the vampires were there and in the next they'd faded away into the shadows of the coming dawn.

"I'll recon ahead and be right back." Aodhán strode away, bloody sword held at the ready. In a few minutes he came back, a scowl on his face. He kicked at the legs of one of the downed zombies. "There are at least as many between us and the apartment complex," he said. "And none between us and Maddalene's enclave."

Oh, God. They'd never make it through another horde.

"I guess it's back to Duncan's, then," she whispered.

Duncan's jaw firmed. "No. Until I can guarantee your safety, we won't return there. We'll have to find someplace else to hole up for a while." He turned her and began walking back the way they'd come, Natalie and Aodhán following behind. "I promise you," Duncan said, "I will give my life to protect you all."

But that wasn't what she wanted. She didn't want his death. Glad of Duncan's supporting arm around her waist, she put one foot in front of the other, growing fatigue threatening to pull her under. By the time they'd gone only a block she was ready to drop.

"In here," Duncan said and swooped her up in his arms to carry her the rest of the way. He led them into an abandoned café and set her on a sofa in a corner seating area near the kitchen in the back of the restaurant. "I need to get more help," he murmured. Looking at Aodhán, he said, "Stay here with them. I'll be just a few minutes."

Even knowing they needed reinforcements, she didn't want him going anywhere near Maddalene. "Wait."

"I'll be all right, sweetheart." He pressed a kiss to her mouth. "I'll be right back." Before she could say more, he was gone.

"Get some sleep if you can, *mo chara*," she heard Aodhán say through the fog of her fatigue. She murmured a response and finally allowed sleep to overtake her.

* * *

Duncan kept to the shadows and waited for one of the vampires loyal to him to fetch Atticus. In just a few minutes the former gladiator came through the front gates and joined him.

"Did Maddalene really threaten your safety?" he asked, his tone frosty with disbelief.

Duncan gave an abrupt nod. "We've taken refuge in a café not too far from here. We can talk there."

Atticus grunted his response and they set off, using their vampire speed to eat up the distance in little time. They entered the café and moved to the seating area where Kimber still slept on the sofa.

"Maddalene's out of control." Atticus dropped into one of the chairs at the table where Aodhán and Natalie sat. His silver gaze flicked over them then back to Duncan, who remained standing. He wanted to get to Kimber in an instant if need be. Leaning forward, Atticus braced his elbows on his knees. "It's time, and you know it. Past time, actually."

"Past time for what?" Natalie asked.

Duncan didn't respond, and neither did Atticus. Duncan knew his friend waited for him to acknowledge that Maddalene was no longer deserving of his unswerving loyalty. But to stage a coup…He'd never thought this day would come. Perhaps he'd been naive, or maybe just in denial. Either way, his friend was right. "Yes, it's time."

"Time. For. What?" Natalie shot a glare at him. He noticed when she looked Atticus's way her expression lightened.

Pretty boy.

"Time to remove Maddalene from power." Duncan finally sat in a chair facing Atticus and just as quickly got back to his feet. "We need those loyal to us here. We must strike now."

"Give me half an hour. We'll reconvene here once I have things in place." Atticus left the café.

A low moan sounded from the seating area.

"Keep watch," he said to Aodhán and Natalie. He headed over to Kimber.

Kimber moaned again. Her legs thrashed and her head twisted to one side then the other.

Duncan sat on the edge of the sofa. "Kimber, wake up. You're dreaming." When another groan left her, he leaned over and took her shoulders in a firm grip. "Kimber. Wake. Up."

Her eyes shot open on a gasp. For a few seconds she seemed unaware of her surroundings, then her gaze flickered over his face. "Oh God, Duncan." Tears filled her eyes. She sat up and threw her arms around him, burying her face against his chest. "Something's…different. *I* feel different."

He pressed a kiss to her temple. "What do you mean? How do you feel different?"

"I feel like I normally do after tapping into the Unseen, but there's something more." She heaved a sigh. "I'm not sure I can explain it. God, I can't even tell if this is a good more or a really, really bad more."

He tightened his arms. He felt powerless to help her, much like he'd been when she'd tried to help Bishop. "How did you stop the zombies?"

"You know how I told you the Unseen reached for me that night with Whitcomb? And then again with Bishop? But it was dark? Evil."

He nodded, but realized with her face pressed to his chest she couldn't see his head. "Yes, I remember."

"It was the same tonight. And I thought, maybe I shouldn't fight it, that I should let it grab me." She drew back slightly and looked up into his face. Her hazel eyes sparkled with tears. "So I did, and when I pushed that negative energy out at the zombies, it undid their reanimation. But now I feel different."

He kissed her lips. "I'm sure it's just fatigue, sweetheart." God, he hoped that was all it was. Whatever had happened, they'd deal with it together. "You get more rest, and when you wake up you'll feel better."

She lay back down without complaint. With a sniff she stared up at him. "Duncan, I'm scared."

He leaned over and wiped her tears away with his thumbs. His little warrior, always so indomitable. Her fear ate at his calm. "We'll handle this together, Kimber." He kissed her again, moving his mouth over hers in a soft, gentle caress. "Sleep now. Worry later, all right?"

She gave a nod and her eyes fluttered closed. In another minute her breathing evened out.

He stared down at her. Tonight all their lives could end. Or it could be the beginning of a new era.

One thing he was certain of: he loved Kimberly Treat and would do everything in his power to keep her safe and make her as happy as possible in this crazy apocalyptic world.

Right now, though, he had a queen to overthrow.

Chapter Fourteen

An hour later, Duncan and Atticus stood side by side and looked over the vampires gathered in Duncan's large living room. He'd left Aodhán and Natalie with a still-sleeping Kimber at the café and had sent several vampires loyal to him to help guard her and his friends. Duncan and Atticus had put the final touches on their plan while hunkered down in the restaurant and had returned to Maddalene's compound mere minutes ago.

He hated that it had come down to this. But he had to admit—and hopefully not too late—that Maddalene had been on a downward spiral for at least the last decade. After Eduardo's true death she'd gotten worse.

Eduardo had been a sadistic bastard, but he'd been fair. Reasonable. And he'd somehow managed to tamp down Maddalene's aggression and irrational tendencies. Since he'd been gone... Well, Duncan himself had been a recipient of her out of control behavior, hadn't he?

Now he looked across a room filled with nearly fifty vampires, all male. It didn't surprise him that the women had sided with Maddalene, even though Atticus had expressed surprise. He'd been sure they'd have some of the females on their side.

It didn't matter. When it came down to it, male vampires were stronger than females, and they needed the brute strength if this was going to work.

"Where is she right now?" Duncan asked, keeping his voice low. They still had guards posted outside in the hallway, but he didn't want to take a chance of someone listening in and reporting back to the queen.

"In her suite," Atticus said. His silver eyes glittered with eagerness for battle. "You know her supporters will fight to the death."

"As will we," one of the vampires said.

Duncan looked his way.

"We've all suffered, one way or another, from Maddalene's lack of foresight. She treats humans as slaves, as pets, as things to be used and discarded, when they should be cared for and protected." He glanced around at the others in the room. "I for one have no desire to try to gain sustenance from animals. We need humans."

"You don't think they taste better if they're scared?" Duncan asked.

The man shook his head. "No, sir. It makes the blood taste sharp. Gamey."

Duncan inclined his head. "I agree. Blood given freely has a much richer taste." He looked around the room. "Atticus and I, along with a select few, will take care of Maddalene. The rest of you... You know what needs to be done." He clapped his hand on Atticus's shoulder. "Let's do this."

In the main hallway, he gave the vampires standing guard in the hallway a lingering look, putting all of his authority in his stare. Motioning toward Maddalene's door, he rumbled quietly, "No one other than Atticus or me gets in, is that understood?"

Each man gave a nod.

"Let's go." Hardening his resolve, he moved forward, Atticus at his side followed by the rest of the rebels. He went still inside for a moment, realizing truly for the first time that he was on the side of this fight he'd never really thought he would be. He'd always been able to talk Maddalene down from whatever potentially disastrous action she'd wanted to take. But taking a whipping at her hand had driven home very succinctly that she no longer listened to him.

They paused outside her door. Atticus looked at him and asked in a low voice, "Ready?"

Duncan nodded. Without bothering to knock, he pushed open the door to her throne room and entered. Atticus and several other vampires followed. Maddalene's four royal guards immediately formed a line between them and their queen.

"What is the meaning of this?" she asked, her manner haughty and disdainful. "You have not been summoned."

Duncan ignored her for the moment and focused his attention on her guards. "Maddalene's rule is over," he told them. "Don't let your vows to protect your ruler with your life end things for you as well."

To a man they straightened their shoulders and scowled. "She is still our leader," one said. "We will adhere to our vows."

"So be it," Atticus growled.

Duncan took the guy to his left, grunting as the guard delivered a hard punch to his ribs. He was aware of the fight going on around him, of Atticus squared off with another guard, and the remaining two royal guards battling it out with four vampires loyal to Duncan. The others remained by the door, watching for a moment when they might be needed, and guarding the door against intruders.

Duncan ducked a hand heading for his jaw and planted his fist in his opponent's gut. He heard a grunt then a low snarl. The vampire came at him, fangs flashing, digging into the arm Duncan threw up to protect his face. Duncan growled at the pain and shook the other vampire off. After several minutes of both of them jockeying for position, he finally saw an opening. He feinted to the left, and as guard left himself open to attack from the right, Duncan pushed forward and sank his teeth into his opponent's throat.

The other vampire thrashed in his hold, but Duncan bit down and held on, and within seconds had drained the guard of enough blood to render him powerless. He let the vamp drop to the floor and turned to assess the situation.

Atticus had defeated his opponent and the other guards were dead as well. That just left Maddalene.

Duncan turned to face her. She stood tall and defiant near the wall of implements of torture she'd used to keep her subjects in line. She wore an air of nobility she no longer deserved. "You dare!" Her eyes flashed silver fire and long fangs curled over her lower lip.

"Only because you've left us no alternative." Duncan rocked back on his heels, willing to bargain with her because of what she'd once meant to him. "Step aside and we'll let you live."

"Duncan." Atticus's low voice was little more than a growl as he came to stand at Duncan's right side. He clearly didn't agree with leaving the queen alive.

"I will never willingly step down." She gave Duncan a once over. "You once held so much promise," she sneered and tossed her hair over her shoulder. "Being around that little human has made you soft. Weak."

Being around Kimber, seeing the kind of strength, both emotional and physical, with which she faced each day, had inspired him. It had made him stronger. Better.

"You're wrong," he answered Maddalene. "My time spent with Kimber and her friends has shown me how things could be. How they *should* be." He took a step forward. "You rule through fear, Maddalene, and it's unnecessary. The world we live in is harsh enough already; there's no need to bring that harshness within these walls."

She lifted her chin. "You're a fool. You speak of harshness." Her eyes narrowed. "Fear and power are what our kind understands. They respond only to strength. And humans…" She trilled a laugh. "Humans are food. They're not friends. Or lovers." She glanced over his shoulder, and he partially turned to follow her gaze to her human attendants who cowered near the chaise. "They're pathetic, weak fools," she said.

As he turned back toward her, she leaped forward, fingers curled, nails ready to rip into his flesh. He reared back, managing to keep his face from being damaged, but couldn't evade her nails raking down his neck. He hissed in pain and slapped her hands aside.

Her answering scream was one of rage. She came at him again, slamming into him with force, taking them both to the floor with bone-jarring desperation. Her eyes flashed silver fire at him; spittle dripped off her fangs as she brought her face closer to his. "You think you can defeat me?" she rasped. "A youngling like you?"

"I must." He wrapped his hands around her upper arms and struggled to hold her away from him. "Your insanity cannot be allowed to continue." He finally was able to gain some traction with his feet and brought them up to shove her off of him.

His effort tossed her halfway across the room, where she landed on her back. She sprung to her feet and, moving with the kind of speed only the oldest of vampires had, was back upon him before he could do much more than stand. He darted to the side and managed to cage her in his arms from behind. Taking advantage of the situation, he bit into her neck where it met her shoulder. Thick, hot blood coursed down his throat, the blood of an ancient, giving him the additional strength he needed to defeat her.

She shrieked and twisted out of his hold. Her gaze, when she met his, held her acknowledgment of what he'd just realized—her blood would contribute to her own downfall. She gave another scream and came at him like a madwoman.

Dodging her outstretched arms, he wrapped one hand around her throat and slammed her against the wall. With his other hand he caught her wrists and held her confined. "Your problem, Maddalene, is that you're overconfident. You think that you were able to whip me because of your authority?" He let his lips pull away from his fangs in a smile. "You whipped me because I allowed it. Because it wasn't yet time to show my hand."

Sounds of fighting bled through the walls. He leaned forward until their faces were inches apart. "Your rule is over. Submit to me and you can find your new place here."

She snarled and fought in his hold like an angry wildcat. "I will never submit!"

"Have it your way." With the hand around her throat he lifted her and slammed her onto the floor. Faster than a blink Atticus knelt on her other side. As one, they bent over her and sank their fangs into her soft, giving throat. Duncan steeled himself against any tender feelings he might have felt toward her. She had saved his life and he had repaid that debt many times over in the last two centuries. While Atticus kept drinking, Duncan lifted his head to stare down into her face.

Her sad yet defiant gaze met his. "If Eduardo had been at my side, you would never have won," she whispered. The light went out of her eyes and her body slumped.

Atticus stood and let out a roar of victory. He grabbed Duncan and yanked him up. "It's over, my friend." He ran his tongue over his teeth, swiping away the last of Maddalene's blood. "Let's get the rest of them under control."

* * *

Two hours later Duncan sat on the steps that led to the platform containing the chaise. They'd won, and he'd never been so exhausted. As his supporters flowed into the room, he pushed to his feet and held up one hand for silence. Once everyone had quieted, he looked out over the gathering. "We fought hard today and won. Let us not lose sight of what we fought for—an end to tyranny. From this day forward, we will build a community of respect. Yes, there will be rules, and there will be strict punishment for breaking those rules, but no longer will we be ruled by fear."

A cheer went up. When it ended, Atticus said, "By vampire law, the second-in-command is the successor to the king or queen. Duncan, however, has asked that you choose who is to lead us."

"Duncan!" one voice shouted.

"Why don't you lead us, Atticus?" someone else asked.

He shook his head. "I am not a leader, my friends. Not like that. Give me a battalion and I'm happy. Give me the entire army and I'll be miserable. As would everyone else very soon."

Laughter sounded.

Duncan called for attention. "Let's have your vote, then," he said. "Who do you pick to lead you?"

His name echoed through the chamber and satisfaction filled him. He could do this. He would do this. And the first thing he would change was the way humans were viewed.

"We will have two new humans under our roof tonight—Kimberly Treat and Natalie Lafontaine. They are personal friends of mine and from this point forward have sanctuary here." He looked out over the group. "They are not to be harmed."

Heads nodded in affirmation.

"Zachary, would you please take those two," he motioned to the former queen's attendants, "and make sure they rest and are cared for?"

"Of course." A dark-haired vampire walked over to the two

men who, after exchanging a few words, rose to their feet and followed him out of the room.

Duncan dismissed the rest of the vampires and sank back onto the steps. Atticus sat down beside him. "Report," Duncan murmured.

"We lost fifteen. All of Maddalene's followers are accounted for. Dead," he added before Duncan could ask. Atticus rolled his shoulders. "I've been waiting for this for so long, it hardly seems real." He glanced down at his bloodied clothing. "Well, except for this."

Duncan grimaced. Human coups were rarely bloodless. Vampire coups were *never* bloodless. He'd been sincere in offering Maddalene a place here even while he'd known she would never accept. She'd always had an excess of pride.

"Something else we've been talking about," he said to Atticus. "I'm putting you in charge of recruiting. We need humans here. They will eat well and be taken care of, and in return they will offer their blood. Emphasize to recruits that it is mostly a painless process and they will give no more than they would at a blood drive like hospitals and charitable organizations used to hold."

Atticus nodded. "You can count on me."

Duncan snorted. "With that pretty face we'll probably be overrun with humans wanting to be donors." He smiled at Atticus's dark frown. "Just don't be too successful, all right?" He clapped a hand to his friend's shoulder and sobered. "Thank you for your support and friendship, Atticus. I couldn't have done this without you."

"Ah, hell. Who's being all pretty now?" His grumbling was belied by the twinkle of humor in his eyes. "Go get your woman. I'll mop up here."

Duncan stood and watched as his friend went over to the back wall and pulled down a sword. He walked over to Maddalene's body and, powerful muscles flexing, he sliced through her neck.

Gritting his jaw, Duncan left the room. He knew the beheading was necessary—it was the only way to ensure Maddalene would never be revived. Someone should have done that to Eduardo, but of course Maddalene would never have allowed it.

He took a quick shower and dressed in clean clothes. Ten minutes later he walked through the front door of the café and smiled to see Kimber sitting up and looking alert. She had color in her cheeks and clarity in her eyes. He went to one knee beside her and clasped her hands. "You look better. How're you feeling?"

"Better." She gave a soft smile. "Still a little tired." Her gaze searched his face. "Aodhán and Natalie filled me in on what was going on."

"Yeah, we pretty much had to sit on her to keep her from running to the compound to help," Natalie said with a snort.

Kimber grimaced. "I was worried."

He lifted her hand and pressed a kiss to her soft palm. "Your worry was a useless expenditure of energy, sweetheart. We won. Maddalene is dead."

"It's about time," she muttered. She stroked her fingers down his cheek. "And you're all right?" She leaned back a little. "You look all right, but you're not hurt?"

"I'm fine." He drew her to her feet and planted a quick, hard kiss on her mouth. "But let's get to the compound now and away from zombies. We can catch up once we're secure."

Duncan led the group back to the enclave, glad to be able to make the trip with only a few zombies in the way, easily dispatched by the cadre of guards. The guards split away from them once they entered the main gates, and Duncan, Kimber, Natalie, and Aodhán proceeded to his suite.

In the aftermath of the battle, a dozen vampires stood guard in the hallway. He beckoned four of them into his quarters. "I'd like you to stand guard inside on either side of the door. For the time being, only Atticus is allowed access to these rooms. If anyone other than him gets in, kill them."

The four guards nodded.

Natalie sighed and plopped into a chair, her legs straight out, arms hanging on either sides of the chair. Duncan walked down the hallway, his hand at the small of Kimber's back, and pushed open the door to the bedroom, guiding her inside. Now that it was all over, he felt like he could sleep for a week. After he made love to Kimber for a week. Or a lifetime. But there were other matters to be taken care of first. He helped her get settled onto the bed and pulled the covers over her. She was still exhausted, and the trip from the café had taken a lot out of her. Her eyes drooped and within seconds she was asleep again.

"So I'll be going, then." Aodhán paused inside the doorway.

"Going?" Natalie yelled from the living room. She appeared behind Aodhán. "Going where?"

"Back to my people, lass." Aodhán kept his voice low and looked at Duncan. "The only reason I've stayed as long as I have is because I promised you I'd look after Kimber. Now there's no more need." He paused. "I assume she and Nat will be staying here."

"Yes." Duncan scrubbed the back of his neck. "The vampires who support me have the same philosophy as I do about humans. Kimber and Natalie have been given sanctuary here. Everyone here recognizes the sanctity of that promise."

"Good." Aodhán turned to Natalie and without another word yanked her into his arms. One big hand cradled the back of her head and the other clamped onto her ass to haul her as close as he could get her. His mouth slammed down onto hers.

Duncan watched with one brow raised. He'd known there was attraction between the two, but Aodhán had never acted on it beyond verbal taunting and a kiss here or there. Nothing like this. This...

This was a kiss good-bye.

When Aodhán released Natalie she staggered. He held her until she was steady, then stroked his fingers down her cheek. "Be safe, *mo chroí*." He turned away from her and clasped hands with Duncan. His bright blue eyes burned with regret and determination. "Take care of yourself, my friend." He turned toward Kimber and leaned over her to plant a kiss on her cheek. She never stirred. "Good-bye, *mo chara*." Aodhán's lips curved with a slight smile and he walked out without a backward glance.

Duncan glanced at Natalie to see a tear drip down one cheek. "That's it?" she asked, bewilderment lining her forehead. "He's leaving, just like that?" Her face hardened and small fists clenched. "The hell he is." She stormed out of the room and Duncan heard her yell, "Aodhán, you big freaking fairy bastard! Get back here."

With a smothered grin, Duncan turned back toward the bed

and saw Kimber staring at him with wide eyes. "Why do you do that?" she asked in a soft voice.

"Do what?" He sat on the edge of the bed and smoothed her hair away from her face. Those few minutes of a catnap she'd just gotten weren't nearly enough. She still looked drowsy.

"Fight smiling." She twined her fingers through his where he'd left them resting against her face and pressed her lips to his palm. "You're so gorgeous when you smile. It makes me giddy."

"I haven't had a lot to smile about." He bent and kissed her, a gentle meeting of lips. "Until you."

"Well, I plan to make you smile a lot," she whispered. She looped her arms around his neck. "What's happened since I passed out?"

"Not much," he said, anticipation tightening his muscles. "You know that Maddalene is dead and I'm the new king of the enclave. Sadly, Aodhán has left to return to his people." He grinned at her openmouthed expression. "Oh, and Natalie may have followed him. I don't know about that yet."

Her mouth snapped closed and her eyes narrowed. "Not much has happened, huh?" She smacked him in the chest but returned to her loose hold around his neck. "I'll get you for that."

His grin widened. Her pupils dilated and her breath quickened. "I wouldn't call this giddy," he murmured.

"You wouldn't?"

He shook his head. "I'd call this aroused." He drew her into his arms and slanted his mouth over hers. He slipped his tongue into her mouth, stroking in slowly, tempting her to follow as he retreated. When he pulled back, her breath came in gasps.

Her nipples were tight little beads. He thumbed across one,

feeling its hardness through the layers of her clothing. She moaned. When he looked at her, he saw the fatigue clouding her eyes, saw it in the shadows beneath her eyes and in the paleness of her cheeks. They'd have time for sex later. Right now it was time for giving and receiving comfort.

He stretched out and drew her against him, fitting her back and buttocks against his chest and groin. With her head pillowed on one of his biceps, he settled his other arm across her waist, letting his hand cup her breast. "How do you feel?" he asked.

"Tired," came her prompt reply. "And a little…off. Different."

"So still the same as before?" he asked.

She nodded against his arm. "But I'm too tired to worry about it right now."

He pondered that then said, "I don't want you tapping into the Unseen again, Kimber," he murmured. "It's too dangerous."

"What about the connection you wanted?" came her sleepy reply.

He was silent a moment, thinking about it. He'd held on to the hope from the time he'd first met Kimber and realized what a powerful ability she had. But after seeing what had happened after she'd tapped into it for Bishop and then again several hours ago, he wasn't willing to risk her life. A thought struck him and he turned it over in his mind. He'd wanted a connection to the Unseen so that he could begin to feel again, to experience life the way he had as a human. But he had been, slowly but surely, over the last six months.

Since he'd designated himself as Kimber's protector and had been spending more time with her, all of his emotions had bourgeoned to life. Anger, frustration, irritation were all more acute when dealing with her sass. And happiness, contentment and optimism when dealing with her love and humor.

"I have that connection through you, sweetheart." His heart felt full. He cleared his throat of the emotion obstructing it and placed a kiss in the curve of her neck. God, she felt so good in his arms. So right. "That's all I need."

She wiggled against him like a puppy happy with its master's praise. "That's nice," she whispered. After a few minutes she said, "But I think I need to connect again, Duncan. You saw what I did. That was on a small scale. What if I could do it on a larger scale?"

"No." Absofuckinglutely not. "You could have died. Would have died if you hadn't stopped when you did. We'll survive this, Kimber. We're safe here now."

She was silent as she apparently thought that over. Finally she replied, "But I don't think it would be as bad if other necromancers were helping me."

"I've been told more than once that you're the best, sweetheart. Can others even do what you've done?"

She shrugged, her shoulder blade rubbing against his chest with the movement. "I don't know, but I have to try."

He pressed another kiss to her neck. "If you think you can end the apocalypse, I'll help you." He'd damn well make sure she stayed safe, too. She was his now. He was hers. "Whatever our future holds, we'll face it together."

**Please see the next page for a first look at the next book in the
Awakening Series...**

Vampire's Thirst

Chapter One

Duncan MacDonnough scrubbed his hand over his chin and stared at his second-in-command. Frustration and irritation made his eyes burn and his fangs elongate. "I don't need this right now, Atticus." He tried his best to look stern but feared he came across as whiningly imploring. Not the attitude a newly minted leader of vampires should have. "Tell me you're not serious."

"Sorry, no can do. I am serious." Marcus Atticus shrugged broad shoulders and slouched down into one of two plush dark brown leather armchairs in front of Duncan's wide mahogany desk. The desk faced the large windows in what had been the former queen's throne room but now served as Duncan's office.

The vampire enclave was housed in one of the multi-story buildings of a refurbished tire factory in Akron, Ohio. While the appearance of the outside of the building remained the same from Maddalene's long and autocratic rule, the inside had seen some changes, not the first of which was the room in which Duncan and Atticus now sat.

The plush chaise the queen had used to lounge on, along with her beefy human consorts, was gone. And good riddance. Duncan still bore some scars on his back from the whipping Maddalene had given him, chained to the central post in the middle of the room, over his choosing to be loyal to his human lover instead of his vampire queen. The marks weren't as bad as she'd meant them to be only because he'd been able to feed soon after the beating.

But still, yeah. Good riddance. To more than the damned chaise.

Atticus tapped the fingers of one hand on the wide arm of his chair. "Most of the humans who have signed up to live here as…donors…are fine with staying with the vamps they're assigned to. But a few have decided it's too dangerous—they're afraid their chosen benefactors will be more likely to lose control if their food source is too close—so instead they want to stay within the area we've assigned to new human arrivals."

"I don't have an issue with that." Duncan's hold on his already strained patience began to unravel, and he forced himself to remain calm. This was Atticus, his best friend and someone he knew would always look out for him. He didn't deserve Duncan taking out his frustrations on him. "Why are you acting like it's a problem?" Duncan asked.

"Because they're inciting unrest. Most of them are fine. They understand the danger on the outside. But there are a few who say they don't like being cooped up, unable to leave the compound. They feel like prisoners." The other vampire scowled. "They want to go to the park; can you believe that?"

Duncan stared at Atticus. There were times, and lately those times were coming more and more often, that he just didn't get humans. "The closest one is Glendale Park, and that's at least a mile and a half away. Don't they understand that if they leave the compound they run the risk of being overrun by zombies?" He rubbed a hand over his face. "Is a walk in the park worth it?"

The other vampire lifted one shoulder in a negligent shrug. "They want a vampire escort for protection."

Duncan snorted. Was this what his life had been reduced to? Listening to petty gripes all day long? No wonder Maddalene had been such a bitch. "They can want all they like. I'm not risking anyone unnecessarily just because humans with cabin fever want to take a stroll." He gestured toward the wide window that faced a courtyard between buildings. They'd established a sturdy fence around the courtyard and had vamps on guard 24/7. "They can walk there."

"They say it's not the same."

"Well, I suppose a mile and a half zombie run would give them plenty of exercise." Duncan grinned. "Hmm. Maybe I should re-think this."

Atticus gave a snort. "Don't encourage them." He paused, another scowl turning down his mouth. "One of them punched Natalie in the face this morning."

"What?" Duncan surged to his feet. Natalie Lafontaine was the best friend of his lover Kimber Treat and, over the last several months, had become his friend as well. While he had a duty to keep the humans in his care secure, Kimber and Natalie were the two to whom he was especially committed to maintaining their safety. That Natalie, acting as a liaison between humans and vampires, would be in jeopardy and attacked by her own kind was a possibility that had never entered his mind. "What the hell! We're giving them sanctuary from zombie hordes," he said, bringing up his hands to tick off a list on his fingers. "We keep them safe, we feed them, we clothe them, and all we ask in return is that they provide nourishment once a week to one vampire only. The amount of blood they give isn't even a quarter of what they'd donate to a blood bank."

"I know, but they're afraid." Atticus hunched forward to clasp his hands between his knees. "Natalie tries to allay their fears, but they don't seem to want to listen." He shook his head. "I get that they're scared of us. We're predators, every last one of us. But we provide safety they have little chance of having outside this compound."

Duncan scrubbed the back of his neck and dropped back into his chair. "Fuck a goddamn duck, Atticus. With the death of Maddalene just a month ago I have enough on my plate keeping our people in line. I don't have time to deal with troublemaking humans, too." He sent a frown his friend's way. "That's why I have you. Deal with it."

"That was the plan all along. I already took care of the son of a bitch who hit Nat. He won't be breathing through his nose for a while. Or taking nourishment except through a straw." Another nonchalant shrug lifted one wide shoulder. "I just wanted to keep you in the loop." He cleared his throat. "So, have things with you and Kimber settled down?"

Duncan shot him a glare. "There was nothing to settle down. We're fine." He did his best to believe it, but his friend was a very discerning man.

"Uh-huh." Atticus cocked his head to one side, his silver eyes missing nothing.

Damn him. The former Roman gladiator was over 2,000 years old, not that he'd ever given Duncan an exact birth date. Maybe he was so old he didn't exactly remember. It happened sometimes.

Those silver vampire eyes narrowed on him now. "She's acting like she's in perpetual PMS, my friend. Something isn't right, and don't try to tell me otherwise."

Duncan fought the flinch that wanted to work its way over his face. Kimber had been getting more and more aggressive, and he couldn't help but think that reason was that small amount of the Unseen that had lodged in her soul. He was worried that the Unseen, that mystical force that had once helped her reanimate corpses in her job as a necromancer—and very possibly had, through her, started the zombie apocalypse—would somehow overtake her innate goodness. But what kind of leader would he be if he let that worry show, even to his most trusted friend?

He folded his arms across his chest. "Oh, for fuck's sake, Atticus. Just what the hell would you know about PMS, anyway?"

"I know about women," came the smug reply.

Duncan couldn't argue with that one. It seemed any female, vampire or human, had to only take one look at Atticus and become mindless with lust. He wasn't sure how much of that was Atticus himself and how much of it was due to his age. The longer a vampire lived the more powerful he became. And power took on all sorts of forms, including sexual attraction. Atticus had that to spare. If it weren't for having Kimber in his life, Duncan could have been jealous of the other vampire's easy sway over women.

But he had Kimber. For the moment, anyway. Over the last few weeks while he'd been solidifying his hold over the enclave, he'd sensed her drawing away from him emotionally. Physically they were still as attracted as ever, but there was something she held back from him, some part of herself she didn't want him to see. How could they truly be together if she wouldn't be fully open to him?

Atticus pushed to his feet, drawing Duncan's attention. "I'm going to check on Natalie," his second-in-command murmured. "And maybe get a bite to eat while I'm there." He winked then tipped his head toward the closed door that led into the hallway. "Kimber's coming."

Duncan caught her scent just as the door swung open. He shot a glance at his friend. "Keep me posted."

"You bet." Atticus paused beside the redhead standing just inside the doorway and pressed a kiss to her cheek. "Hey there, sweetheart."

"Atticus." She smiled and patted his shoulder. "Nat was looking for you."

"Just on my way to see her." He closed the door behind him.

Kimber clicked the lock in place and walked toward Duncan.

He stood and moved around to the front of his desk, resting his buttocks on the edge, and watched her move farther into the room. She wore her usual T-shirt and jeans, both garments hugging her slim curves. His body reacted as it always did; his cock began to harden, his fangs elongated, lust and love burned his eyes.

Her auburn hair fell to her shoulder blades, longer than it had been when this whole mess had started, longer than when he'd first met her over a year ago. Her hazel eyes met his and a slow smile curved her full lips.

"I know that look," he murmured and drew her into a loose embrace. Clasping his hands at the small of her back, he pulled her between his spread legs.

"What look would that be?" She pressed a kiss to his chin, his jaw, just beneath his ear. Her hands lifted, fingers threading through his hair, the light tugs zinging straight to his balls.

A shudder of need worked its way through his body. He took her mouth with his, deep, hard, a kiss of possession. Of being possessed. Breaking the kiss, he stared into her eyes. "The look that says you want me and mean to do something about it."

"Damn straight." Her smile widened. "I'm here for a nooner." She pressed her lips to the indent at the base of his throat. She undulated against him, her belly slowly grinding against his erection.

"It's one o'clock in the morning," he managed to say on a groan. Until Kimber, no woman before had been able to drive his desire so high so fast.

"Well, since you don't usually start work until after dark, and sunset was at 8:30, this is your noon."

"I have a one-thirty appointment." He cupped her ass and dragged her fully against him, letting her feel the rigid length of his cock against her belly. She moaned and deepened the kiss, driving her tongue into his mouth, winding it around his own in an ancient dance of pleasure and need. She leaned into him, pressing into the space between his legs, and he cupped her against him.

"This won't take long," she murmured against his lips. She yanked at the waistband of his pants, unbuttoning and unzipping and getting his pants and underwear around his thighs so his hard cock sprang free. She gripped him, sliding her hand from base to tip, and slid her thumb across the sensitive tip.

He groaned. "Too many clothes," he muttered, fingers working at the button at the waistband of her jeans. He wanted her naked. Now. He shoved her jeans and panties over her hips and pushed them to her ankles. She toed off her shoes then kicked out of the garments pooled around her ankles. With a wiggle and a smile she drew her shirt over her head, letting it fall to the floor.

Duncan made quick work of getting Kimber out of her bra and stared at her a moment. "God, you're beautiful," he rasped. He leaned forward and swiped his tongue over one of her nipples, then the other, and straightened to see them tighten into hard, puckered nubs. "Sit where I am," he said, his voice rough as he moved to give her his place on the edge of the desk.

She arched a brow but did as he asked, perching on the wooden surface. "Okay, but I'm going to mess up your desk. I'm already wet." She wriggled a bit, trying to get comfortable.

"I hope so." He dragged a chair to where she sat, then even closer, between her splayed legs. As he took his place, he looked up at her for a moment, and it was clear she knew his intent. Already her breath came unsteadily as she moved closer to the edge to grant him greater access to the soft folds between her thighs. She leaned back on her hands, breasts thrusting up.

With his hands just inside her knees, he spread her legs wider and looked at the pussy before him. She was pink and wet and swollen. *His.* The musk of her desire perfumed the air, that sweetly spiced scent that was uniquely Kimber. He placed his thumbs on the outer lips of her sex and spread her open before he lowered his mouth to taste her. As he lazily traced her with the tip of his tongue, being careful not to nick her with his fangs, she gasped and jolted, and gripped at the desk top. He covered her clit for a moment, sucking the sensitive bud of nerves into his mouth, rolling it gently between his teeth. Her gasps and moans grew louder, the sweetest sounds he'd ever heard.

"Duncan!" She bucked up into his mouth, demanding in her need. "Stop fooling around and make me come."

Demands he ignored. He built her pleasure, taking her higher and higher, then backing off, then once more ratcheting up her pleasure until she fell apart in his arms. He left her clit and languidly licked her slit over and over. As he found a rhythm, stroking her entrance with firm swipes of his tongue, she lifted her hips against him, moaning, propped up on her elbows.

He focused once more on her abandoned clit, swirling his tongue around the bud first with light pressure, then increasing it bit by bit, swipe by swipe until she was shaking, just on the edge of orgasm.

With a moan of his own he sucked her hard and pressed two fingers deep into her sheath. She dropped flat on her back, her hips lifting off his desk, a scream of pleasure erupting from her throat that likely was heard throughout the complex. Her hips bucked. He continued his sensual torment even after her butt rested once more against the desk, her breasts rising with her gulping breaths. Only when she was finally still did he push the chair back and stand.

Before he could turn her over to take her from behind, she slid off the desk. "I want you inside me." She put her hands on his shoulders. "Now. I want to ride you."

Even as he wondered anew at her aggression, in this instance he thought it wasn't such a bad thing. He grinned and went down on his knees, then his back. She came down over him, knees on either side of his hips. One slender hand gripped his erection and pointed it where she wanted him. She dropped onto him, taking him deep with one smooth movement. She cried out and bucked with a second orgasm almost immediately. He clasped her hips, holding her where he wanted her, and thrust up, fighting his way in and out of her swollen flesh with no thought beyond wanting to explode with blinding release. The base of his spine tingled and his balls drew up tight against his body. At the moment his orgasm gripped him, his release jetting into her wet heat, he reared up and sank his fangs into the softness of her throat. She jerked and cried out, then as the pain of the bite faded she gave a low, needy moan.

Her blood tasted rich and salty. *His.* This incredible woman was his.

Slender fingers clutched at him, nails digging into his shoulders. The slight sting of pain enhanced his passion, and he drank a little deeper. She moaned with pleasure, another climax rocketing through her. When it was done, he licked over her wound and wrapped his arms around her, holding her naked body close, clinging to her. For these few brief moments, his heart beat and his body and mind soared with pleasure so powerful he could do nothing more than shudder against her.

"I love you." Her words were so soft he almost missed them. And that was saying something, since as a vampire he had a heightened sense of hearing.

Keeping his cock firmly embedded in her slick channel, he

gently pushed her shoulders back so he could look into her eyes. Sliding his hands from her shoulders, he cupped her face. Her lovely, sweet face. "That's the first time you've said it," he murmured and dropped a kiss against the corner of her mouth.

Her eyes were dark, glittering with an emotion he couldn't decipher. It looked almost like...anger. Maybe even hate. But he didn't sense those emotions from her. All he felt from her was affection. And the love she professed.

"You've never said it, either," she rejoined, her voice soft yet still holding a thin thread of steel.

He frowned. "Sure I have."

She shook her head. "No, you haven't. I've been listening very hard for those three words, and you've never said them."

"I've felt them, Kimber." Duncan kissed her, a lingering melding of lips, of hearts. "I do love you. So much."

She wrapped her arms around his waist and hugged him. She yawned, her breasts rubbing against his shirt. After a few minutes she lifted off him, and he let loose a growl of complaint at the sense of loss he felt when his cock left the haven of her body. She gave him a saucy grin and a quick kiss on one corner of his mouth. "You want more, you'll have to come across the hall." She got to her feet and stared down at him, passion written all over her face, in the tense stance of her slender body. "You should come with me now. I want you again."

He wished he could, but his next appointment was important. He shook his head as he stood. He righted his clothing, tucked his cock into his pants and zipped up. "I have a meeting with Xavier. I can't cancel it."

Annoyance and that ever present aggression flashed in her

eyes, turning the hazel to a vibrant green before she tamped it down with an effort he could see. "I know," she said, her eyes hazel once more. She took a breath, as if fighting for control, and pressed a slender hand to his cheek. "I realize this partnership is important. If we can establish a safe corridor between here and Cleveland, all of us will be more secure and better able to get supplies."

He helped her get dressed, though it took longer than it would have if she'd been on her own. Every few seconds he had to pause to stroke and kiss. When she was finally clothed, she seemed to have her emotions under control. With a teasing expression she clucked her tongue and stared at him. "You didn't even take off any of your clothes."

He grinned. "That's the advantage men have, I suppose."

She rolled her eyes. "Well, when you decide to come to bed, you may find that advantage won't work for you there." She went on her tiptoes and pressed a soft kiss against his mouth, then moved away. Heading toward the door, she sent him a look over her shoulder full of promise. "See you later."

"Count on it."

After she'd gone, Duncan walked back around his desk and sat down. He could feel the grin on his face and knew he probably looked like a lovelorn sap, but he didn't care.

She loved him.

Finally, Kimber Treat loved him.

About the Author

Many writers will tell you they began writing stories the moment they learned to wield a pencil. My own first story was written in sixth grade at the behest of my teacher to write a story with this opening phrase: "It was a dark and stormy night." But even as a child, I didn't write "kid" stories. I preferred something darker, something that went bump in the night.

As I grew older, I began to read various genres. I especially enjoyed fantasy and science fiction along the lines of J.R.R. Tolkien and Ray Bradbury. I discovered Bram Stoker and Arthur Conan Doyle.

Then I came across romance. Not only could I have fantasy, alien, horror, or mystery, I could also get a great boy-gets-girl story as well. I was hooked. And along with the passion for reading romance came a passion for writing it as well. After moving to Arizona and working a hectic job for a few years, I joined Romance Writers of America and in 2005 decided to get serious about writing as a career. I was able to take a year off work to focus on my writing. I began with novella-length paranormal stories that I had published with electronic publishers such as Ellora's Cave, Amber Heat, and Liquid Silver Books (under the pen name Sherrill Quinn).

A few years later I sold a werewolf series (also under the name Sherrill Quinn) to Kensington, and in 2012 my Warriors of the Rift series (written as Cynthia Garner) found its home at the Forever imprint of Grand Central Publishing. Most recently I sold a two-part vampire series to Forever Yours, and I hope there are many more to come!